She v[...]
Nicos on Parnassos

Her head felt light and her heart began to beat madly against her breast. Was she falling in love?

She pushed the thought away from her, but it was still there when they finally climbed higher to see the little temple from a different viewpoint.

They did not speak, standing there, hand in hand. The stillness, the sense of awe in the hushed atmosphere, wrapped around them, drawing them close, and at last he drew her fully into his arms.

"Rhea, you've made it all new for me," he said quietly.

She stood in the circle of his imprisoning arms as he kissed her, and she gave him back kiss for kiss, passionately and unreservedly, without thought, her senses swimming as his dark head blotted out the brilliance of the sun.

Jean S. MacLeod, the author of more than fifty romance novels, lives with her husband on an isolated peninsula in Scotland's Western Highlands. From her doorstep she has a breathtaking view of the Hebrides. "In these surroundings," she says, "it must surely be possible to go on writing for a very long time." Indeed, her ideas and words are as fresh and romantic as ever.

Books by Jean S. MacLeod

HARLEQUIN ROMANCE

Don't miss any of our special offers. Write to us at the following address for information on our newest releases.

Harlequin Reader Service
901 Fuhrmann Blvd., P.O. Box 1397, Buffalo, NY 14240
Canadian address: P.O. Box 603,
Fort Erie, Ont. L2A 5X3

The Olive Grove
Jean S. MacLeod

Harlequin Books

TORONTO • NEW YORK • LONDON
AMSTERDAM • PARIS • SYDNEY • HAMBURG
STOCKHOLM • ATHENS • TOKYO • MILAN

Original hardcover edition published in 1986
by Mills & Boon Limited

ISBN 0-373-17009-2

Harlequin Romance first edition March 1988

CHAPTER ONE

THE necklet lay on the table as Rhea Langford packed the remainder of her belongings into the cases she was taking with her to Greece. Should she leave the necklet here, she wondered, or should she take it back to the land of its origin where it seemed to belong?

The pale spring sunshine, striking through the window of the Pimlico flat which she had shared with two other girls during the years when she had trained as a physiotherapist, picked out the delicate tracery of the gold banding which linked the stones, and each stone shone with its own particular brilliance; blood red and sapphire blue, and yellow, like an evil eye, and a pale, clear amethyst like the waters in a shallow bay.

'You'll be taking this, I suppose.'

Rhea looked up at her flat-mate, realising that she had almost forgotten Janice in her preoccupation with the future.

'I'm not sure,' she said, 'but it does seem to belong there.'

'As you do,' Janice Grant suggested. A tall girl with a long mane of flowing hair, she had been closer to Rhea than any of the others during the time they had shared the flat. 'You've spoken so much about Greece and it does seem to be your second home. I've often wondered why you didn't go there when your grandparents died.'

'There were so many other things to do.' Rhea hesitated. 'I had promised them to finish my training, for one thing, and—I hadn't really any close contact with my mother's people. Athens seemed so far away and I didn't even speak their language, though I had written to my cousin from time to time. She was still at school then and eager to perfect her English, but now she's eighteen and waiting to go to college later in the year.'

'Well, then, you have this cousin to fall back on,' Janice pointed out. 'Ariadne, wasn't it?'

5

'Ariana,' Rhea corrected her. 'It's such a pretty name, I think, and I hope we are going to be friends in spite of the difference in our ages.'

'Of course, being twenty-two does age you!' Janice smiled. 'Continental girls grow up more quickly than we do and marry younger, I believe, so you may even find Cousin Ariana to be completely worldly-wise. Was your mother very young when she met your father out there?'

Rhea lifted the necklet from the table, holding it thoughtfully for a moment before she answered.

'I believe so. I also know that she was very beautiful and my father was very much in love with her. He gave her this.' She looked down at the necklet in her hands. 'It was a sort of love token, a copy of an ancient torque which had been found on a "dig" on one of the Aegean islands while he was working there. Archaeology was his great obsession and he went to Greece whenever he could. He made a great many friends there, but when he married he brought my mother back to London where he was employed in shipping. It was a Greek line, so perhaps that was why he had so many ties with Athens.' She carried the necklet to the window where she continued to look at it as if it embodied all the past for her and some of the future. 'I've always wondered about Greece—what I should find there if I ever went— perhaps the other half of myself,' she mused. 'My mother died when I was five years old and I was brought up by my father's parents in Cumberland, so I never really knew my mother's people. I met them once when I was about four, but I hardly remember them, and after my mother died my father never wanted to go to Greece again.'

'He didn't marry again?'

'No.' Rhea straightened, turning back from the window to lay the necklet on the table again where the sun caught it in a noose of light. 'He remained faithful to her memory till he died, and when I was eighteen he gave me this.' She touched the necklet lovingly. 'I'll never part with it, Janice, as long as I live. I know it's only an imitation of the real thing, but to me it means all his love and devotion through the years when I was growing up.'

'To be the image of your mother?'

Rhea shook her head.

'I don't think so,' she smiled. 'My mother was classically beautiful and I'm like my father's mother, as a matter of fact, and I can't quarrel with that. She was the kindest person I've ever known.'

'Your Greek grandmother could be equally kind,' Janice suggested. 'After all, she has invited you to go out there and meet the family now that you have no definite ties here. You told me the other day that there was nothing to stop you doing what you wished to do for at least a year before you started your career in earnest. It isn't as if——' Janice hesitated for a moment, going on deliberately to make a point which had troubled her in the past. 'It isn't as if you're still carrying a torch for Robert Dearne. He wasn't worth all the tears you spent on him, Rhea. Not one little bit.'

'I know that,' Rhea acknowledged. 'I know that now, but it was a first experience, Jan—a bitter let-down, you could say.' Her voice was not quite steady. 'It shook my faith in people—and love—for a very long time.'

'I know,' her flat-mate acknowledged. 'But I'm glad you're cured.'

Was she 'cured'? Rhea could not answer truthfully because, even now, her heart felt bruised by the experience of loving and being rejected so cruelly by someone she had trusted completely. When Robert Dearne had walked away and married someone else without telling her she had been devastated and only the friendship and understanding of her flat-mates had helped her to bridge the gap between then and now. She believed herself 'cured', but she knew that some of the heartache would remain with her for a very long time. It would caution her if love ever looked her way again.

'Do you want me to run you to Heathrow?' Janice asked, dismissing the past in the urgency of the present.

'I was going to phone for a taxi——'

'No need. I have the day off and nothing pleases me

more than seeing people starting out on a romantic journey,' Janice declared. 'How long will you be away?'

'A month—perhaps two.' Rhea looked uncertain. 'It will all depend on what I find when I get there.'

'Rhea,' Janice said, 'you're going to the other half of your family!'

'Whom I hardly know,' Rhea pointed out.

'Isn't there something about blood being thicker than water?' Janice asked dismissively. 'Stop worrying about how you'll be received and enjoy yourself. You can always come back.'

On the way to the airport Rhea felt in her handbag for the necklet, because now it seemed to be some sort of amulet to safeguard the future. The original torque had been buried beneath the soil of an Aegean island for hundreds of years to be restored to the light of day by her father many years ago, and now the replica was in her keeping as she carried it back to the fair land of its origin.

Her first flight of any distance was over almost before she realised it, and they were coming in to land at Athens with a whole panorama of sea and mountains and islands glistening in the sun under the cloudless Aegean sky. It seemed that she could see for miles, far, far beyond the islands and the sea to other, distant mountains pale on the horizon's rim while her eager thoughts rushed ahead of her to her first meeting with Ariana Karousis who was her cousin and eager correspondent of the past few weeks. 'Wear something green,' Ariana had suggested, 'although I am sure to recognise you from your photograph.'

Rhea tucked the emerald green scarf into the pocket of her grey cotton dress, carrying her coat because she no longer needed its extra warmth. It had been cold enough for a coat on her way to Heathrow, the chill spring day not yet bright enough to discard it altogether, but since she had left the roomy airbus behind she had felt the heat of the Grecian sun warm on her back and its caress on her cheeks like a welcoming kiss.

Following the stream of travellers, she collected her

luggage, piling it on to a trolley before she looked about her for a familiar face. In the bustle of arrival people of all nationalities swarmed around her and none of them seemed to be alone, as she was. Little groups gathered as whole families swept their arriving relatives away on a gust of exuberant greetings. Children in their Sunday best with bright ribbons in their hair or little mob-caps to match their cotton dresses perched precariously on their dark curls clutched eagerly at extended hands, while dark-clad elderly women followed closely behind, escorted by an attendant son or daughter who guided them carefully through the crowd. Greek family life, Rhea thought. How warm and kind it seems to be!

Gradually she realised that she was almost alone, the last of the travellers from London yet to be met. What could have happened to Ariana, when she had been so sure that she would be there to meet her?

A man and a tall, elegant girl came across the concourse towards her and for a moment they were looking at each other, as strangers sometimes do, and then the girl turned away to collect her expensive-looking hand-luggage which she had left on one of the benches near the main door. The man's penetrating gaze held Rhea's for a moment longer, the blue luminous eyes in the finely chiselled sun-tanned face faintly curious before he followed his companion to the departure lounge.

The brief encounter left Rhea with a vague sensation of shock, although she had no reason to believe that they would ever meet again. The girl had been perhaps the most beautiful woman she had ever seen, tall and slim and groomed to perfection, her fair hair falling to shoulder length, her face expertly made up to accent the compelling beauty of her sombre brown eyes which gazed straight ahead with a look of absolute confidence, as if their owner were well aware of the impression she made.

Not so her companion. He had been taller than the girl he escorted, with the magnetic good looks and obvious virility found in the high noon of Greek sculpture, and the blue eyes set wide in the dramatic face had seemed to challenge the world. A man who had already conquered the world, Rhea thought impartially while she continued her search for her cousin.

A breathless Ariana came running towards her from the main doors, recognising her immediately.

'How sorry I am to be late when we are first met!' she apologised profusely. 'It is not to be easily forgiven, would you say? I have a car that will always let me down when I am in a hurry or have someone important to meet. It has done so today, much to my shame, and there was also difficulty in finding a parking place.' She kissed Rhea warmly on both cheeks. 'You are just what I expected, and you are not angry with me because you are smiling!'

'Why should I be angry,' Rhea asked, returning her embrace, 'when you have come to meet me? My plane may have been a little early.'

'That is very kind,' Ariana acknowledged, 'but Olympic Airways have a pride in arriving to the minute of their schedule. It is I who am at fault. But, Rhea,' she ran on excitedly, 'you must be in need of some refreshment, as I am. We will go to the snack bar and have *tyrópitta* or a *pilaffi*, if you would like that better?'

'I seem to have eaten all the way from London,' Rhea protested, 'but I would very much like something to drink—a coffee, perhaps, while you eat your *tyrópitta*.'

Ariana looked disappointed.

'I wanted so much for you to like our food,' she confessed. 'We eat *tyrópitta* constantly, and it is very good.'

'Well—*tyrópitta* it is!' Rhea laughed. 'Ariana, you can't imagine how good it is to see you!'

Her cousin led her to a small snack-bar in a corner where everyone seemed to be eating what looked like a toasted cheese sandwich, held in a piece of grease-proof paper because it was so hot.

'We'll have our coffee afterwards,' Ariana suggested, leading the way to an empty bench. 'Or perhaps you would prefer some orange juice?'

'Either will do.' Rhea was holding the melted cheese

delicacy away from her cotton dress. 'This is delicious,' she acknowledged. 'No wonder it's so popular.'

'It will do till we reach Volponé,' her cousin agreed, 'then you will have your first truly Greek meal. A family meal,' she added. 'Everybody is wondering about you, Rhea—Grandmama and Grandpapa, and even Aunt Evadne—they are all very curious in their own way, though they will not show it at first. Grandmama does not speak good English, you see, but they will understand what you mean. I have much English,' she added with great pride, 'so we will always speak in your language, unless you want me to help with your Greek?'

Rhea was forced to confess that she had little knowledge of her mother's native tongue.

'Except for a word or two,' she amended.

'You will soon learn,' Ariana told her cheefully, 'though you may find the alphabet confusing at first.'

They ordered two orange juices, drinking them when they had finally disposed of the appetising *tyrópittas* and wiped their fingers on a paper napkin to cope with the grease.

'Oh,' Ariana exclaimed as she set down her cup, 'there's Nicolas! He must be on his way back from somewhere—Corinth or Istanbul, perhaps. He is always travelling from one country to another on business, though he likes best to be at home.'

Rhea turned to meet the newcomer, drawing in a quick breath of surprise as she recognised the man who had looked at her with such a quizzical expression less than half-an-hour ago. This time, however, he was alone. His tall, elegant companion was no longer in evidence as he came purposefully towards them, his deep blue eyes alight with amusement.

'Don't tell me you've come all the way from Volponé in that dreadful contraption I saw in the car-park,' he said to Ariana in English, obviously recognising Rhea's nationality and wishing to be polite. 'I recognised it immediately as the Buggy, of course!'

'It is a perfectly respectable Renault, I would have you know,' Ariana responded with dignity. 'It has hardly ever let me down.'

'You surprise me,' he said, continuing to tease her.

'You are never surprised, Nicolas,' Ariana declared, turning towards Rhea at last. 'But this is my cousin, Rhea, from London, whom you knew we were expecting. She has just arrived and we are on our way to Volponé. Rhea,' she added, forgetting the insult to her mode of conveyance, 'this is Nicolas Metaxas, who lives only a few miles from us on Euboea. He is my grandfather's friend, you understand, although he is much younger than Grandpapa.'

Nicolas Metaxas laughed outright at this careful observation, showing splendid white teeth as he turned towards Rhea.

'That makes a great deal of difference,' he said, his strong fingers closing over hers. 'If you are accepted by Grandpapa Karousis all is well! Seriously, though,' he added, the teasing note fading from his voice, 'I hope you have had a pleasant flight and are not too tired to enjoy the further journey to Volponé.'

'I'm looking forward to it,' Rhea assured him, thinking that no one had the right to be so outstandingly handsome and be gracious into the bargain without a flaw appearing somewhere.

'You've just missed Daphne,' he said. 'She rang and asked me to see her off to Rome on some modelling assignment or other. I wonder she didn't recognise you,' he added to Rhea.

'Daphne would be too concerned with her own affairs,' Ariana put in calmly. 'She hasn't been at Volponé for weeks, and she never seems to be too keen to have me at the flat. Anyway, the old photograph we have of Rhea doesn't do her a bit of justice,' she added generously. 'It was taken just after she left school—when she was about my age—and she has changed a lot, I think. As you know,' she said to Rhea, 'Daphne is also your cousin, but she can not now be called one of the family. She has her own flat in Athens and comes very seldom to the farm. For her,' she added with a brief sigh, 'Volponé is too far or too quiet. She likes always the busy city life and her independence in Athens or Rome.'

It was a severe criticism of her cousin, whom Ariana evidently did not understand, but Nicolas Metaxas did not seem to resent it.

'I was about to offer you a lift since I'm going your way,' he said, glancing again in Rhea's direction, 'but I don't think I dare. Ariana is absurdly attached to her first motor-car, but I feel you would be safer with me.' He took possession of the trolley. 'Let me help you with your luggage, anyway,' he offered.

Walking beside him towards the parking lot, Rhea was aware of an odd feeling of recognition, which was ridiculous when they had never met until now.

'Your grandfather tells me that you have come to stay for some time,' he remarked, 'and no doubt we have much in common. Your father was a keen archaeologist.'

'It was his absorbing hobby. In many ways,' Rhea added, 'it was his whole life.' She turned impulsively towards him as they reached the first line of parked cars. 'He came here quite a lot during his student days. Perhaps you have heard of him finding some of the artefacts on one of the islands.'

'Yes.' He had sounded curiously withdrawn of a sudden. 'I believe he was once my father's friend.'

'It was long before we were born,' Ariana put in thoughtfully. 'Aunt Evadne told me that they worked together on Norbos, but they had a quarrel——'

She broke off regretfully, aware that she had said too much, and Nicolas Metaxas led the way to where a silver-grey convertible glistened in the sun, completely overshadowing the battered little Renault parked beside it. Some of the original warmth had gone out of his voice when he said,

'You're quite sure you won't accept a comfortable lift? It's over two hours' motoring and I could have the Renault picked up and delivered to Volponé in the morning.'

'It won't be necessary to go to so much trouble,' Rhea heard herself saying. 'I'm quite sure we'll manage all right and—no doubt you are in a hurry to get home.'

The blue, luminous eyes held hers for a moment longer with a hint of amusement in their depths.

'No one is ever in a great hurry once they leave Athens behind,' he assured her. 'That is something you will learn very quickly when you reach the country.'

She helped him to load her suitcases into the tiny boot while Ariana took her place behind the steering wheel.

'Thank you,' she said, looking into those magnetic eyes. 'I expect we will meet again while I am at Volponé.'

Ariana started the engine which spluttered twice before it roared into life.

'Get in while the going's good,' Nicolas Metaxas recommended. 'The Buggy doesn't like to be kept waiting!'

He closed the door behind her and it was only then that she realised that he hadn't answered her final question; but perhaps a second meeting at Volponé wasn't quite on the cards.

'Are all Greek men as handsome as that?' she asked her cousin as they drove off.

'Some of them are like Nicolas, but most of them are smaller and darker,' Ariana said after due consideration. 'We are a composite nation, we Greeks, with much foreign blood in our veins, but I always think of Nicolas as a true Greek. I used to believe that he really belonged on Olympus, but I know better now,' she laughed. 'Nicolas is wholly down-to-earth in his attitude to life, although he is the most eligible bachelor in all Attica!'

'Which means he is very rich,' Rhea mused.

'Rich and ambitious,' Ariana agreed, 'but very, very kind, especially if you are in trouble. He has helped me out of a scrape more than once in the past. In my schooldays, you understand. I would not dream of letting him dictate to me now,' she added with true teenage independence.

'You said "ambitious",' Rhea pointed out, displaying too great an interest in a comparative stranger.

'Well—he would like to add to his possessions and buy up more land, although already he has a large estate. But that is Aunt Evadne's estimation,' Ariana added hurriedly. '*I* don't believe Nicolas would be ruthless, even to obtain what he wants most. He is a very loyal person when it comes to friendship, you see.'

'He teases you a great deal,' Rhea remarked. 'Especially about the Buggy.'

'That has always been his way,' her cousin smiled. 'I do not resent it because I know it is all in fun, like—like having an older brother.'

The brief hesitation in her voice made Rhea look at her more closely. Ariana could never be called beautiful in the accepted meaning of the word, but she had a happy little face surrounded by dark, curling hair, and her large brown eyes were full of the joy of living. Standing on the threshold of womanhood, she was eager to embrace all it meant and everything it had to offer, taking happiness and sorrow and even disappointment in her stride.

'Nicolas will not marry for a long time,' she said unexpectedly. 'He has so many things to do.'

Was there disappointment there, or the assurance that her 'true Greek' would wait for her to grow up? Rhea wondered if her cousin was already irretrievably in love with Nicolas Metaxas and was suddenly acutely aware of the other girl he had seen off at the airport, a vision of the immortal Helen of Troy if ever she had seen one. Yet Ariana's smile and attitude were surely too free for that, treating Nicolas more as a brother than a potential conquest for whom she would have to wait. Daphne, the cousin they both shared, had taken an almost proprietary right to him at the airport, but she had no reason to suppose that they were in love.

Speculation about Nicolas Metaxas was absurd, she told herself, however much he may have impressed her. With the bright sunshine of the Attic day pouring down on her and a cloudless sky high above her head, there were other things to absorb her attention as they drove across a wide plain surrounded by majestic mountains and drew near to the city she had longed to see.

Centering round the twin hills of the Acropolis and Mount Lycabettus, Athens skirted their base to spread in every direction, but it was the glory of the Parthenon standing above it all, its honey-coloured columns of

Pentalic marble etched sharply against the deep blue of the sky, which held her enthralled. It remained there, untouchable, away from the crowds, away from the teeming city, aloof and chaste over the years while the life that went on in the plain beneath scarcely seemed to matter. It was supremely beautiful in the strong, bright light of the Athenian day, raised on its high plateau for all to see.

Rhea held her breath as they drove on into the city past squares brightened by flowering orange trees and fountains glittering in the sun with the twin hills as a green and effective backdrop to the white marble façades of chaste and dignified buildings which Ariana attempted to name for her as they passed.

'You have to walk in Athens to see it properly,' she observed, sounding her horn to clear their way of pedestrians who seemed to prefer the middle of the road in order to admire the buildings on either side. 'We'll come again for a whole day's sightseeing just as soon as you've met the family. Even then,' she mused, 'you won't have seen Athens. It will take days—perhaps weeks—and you won't have visited everything.' She steered her way round a magnificent square into a broad and pleasant avenue lined by magnificent old houses adorned with colonnades and faced with Doric porticoes where statues of Athena and Apollo gazed down with indifference at the crawling traffic at their feet. 'We'll come shopping,' she added eagerly, 'and I'll take you to the Pláka where you will see the real Athens. It is said that you should go there by moonlight to truly appreciate it,' she laughed, 'so perhaps Nicolas will take us one evening.' She risked a quick glance at her silent cousin from England. 'You would like that, perhaps?' she asked.

'Oh——!' Rhea roused herself from her sojourn into the past. 'We can't make use of him, Ariana,' she protested for some unknown reason.

'Daphne does!' her cousin declared defensively. 'She is always expecting him to take her out.' She sighed. 'They make a handsome pair, don't you think?'

'Are they engaged to be married?' Rhea asked after the briefest of pauses.

'Oh, no! Neither of them wants to be married just yet,' Ariana decided. 'Daphne has her career and Nicolas is a very busy person who travels a great deal. He has an office in Piraeus, so he is often in Athens where Daphne has her flat.'

'I see.'

Why couldn't she stop wondering about Nicolas Metaxas? Rhea decided to put him out of her immediate orbit to concentrate on the scenery. They were travelling north, away from the centre of the city now, with the undulating foothills of Hymettus bare in the dazzling light of the sun and distant mountains for ever on the horizon. They sped past Byzantine shrines and ancient monasteries grouped under shady chestnut trees on a broad highway from which lesser roads ran off to Marathon and Makri and the myriad little pine-girt beaches that faced the channel and the scattered islands beyond.

Rhea thought about her father and how often he had spoken of this mystic land of legends and gods and heroes; of the gorgons transformed into seductive maidens challenging the captains of ancient caiques to lure them to destruction on the rock-girt shores; of Poseidon, god of the sea, who became Saint Nicolas, the protector of sailors, and Demeter, goddess of plenty, and Orpheus with his lute making music by a stream. Suddenly her father had come very near, travelling with her, it seemed, through this enchanted land where he had found a bride.

'I have so much to learn,' she confessed to Ariana. 'I know so little about my mother's country.'

'Do you know that you have the name of a Greek goddess?' Ariana asked idly. 'Rhea was the mother of Zeus, and she hid him away in Crete because his father, Cronos, gobbled up all his children!'

'She was a brave woman!' Rhea laughed. 'Did he finally gobble her up, too?'

'Oh, no. She was too clever for that,' Ariana declared. 'She lived among the shepherds of Mount Ida for a very long time, protected by Capricorn, the Goat.'

'I'm Capricorn,' Rhea said. 'I was born under that sign.'

'No doubt that was why you were given your name,' Ariana decided. 'Your mother would know all the legends and she would choose your name accordingly. She was my father's sister, you know. They were very happy together when they lived at Volponé as children, but I think you will understand that better when we reach there,' she added. 'It is a beautiful place and our grandparents would never wish to leave it, because it has been their home for a very long time.'

'I can hardly wait to get there,' Rhea confessed. 'Have we much farther to go?'

'Not so very far,' Ariana said, negotiating a sharp bend which the Renault attempted to take in its stride. 'The Buggy doesn't like hills!'

They had turned off the main highway several miles back to enter a well-watered countryside bright with oleanders, and it was here that the wayward little car decided to stop.

'Oh, dear,' said Ariana prosaically. 'Nicolas is going to say "I told you so!" '

'Surely we can start it,' Rhea suggested. 'It was going quite well a moment ago.'

Ariana sighed.

'We can try,' she said, pulling in to the side of the road.

Ten minutes passed as the bright sun slid gently towards the west. It was still very warm, but a breeze from the Channel came up to fan their cheeks as they bent over the raised bonnet of the recalcitrant little vehicle and Ariana did things with a dangerous-looking spanner which she had obviously borrowed from somewhere else.

'I got this from Nicolas,' she explained, 'just in case.'

'Have you broken down before?' Rhea asked, trying to hide her concern.

'Not so far away from home,' Ariana admitted. 'To be honest, I don't know a lot about cars—about their insides, I mean.' She glanced back along the deserted road. 'Someone's sure to come,' she said.

When someone did come it was a man on a donkey-cart, a peasant driving from one village to the next, who seemed equally unacquainted with a car's inside. He looked under the bonnet long and earnestly, however, before he shook his head, regretting his inability to help in a flow of expressive Greek.

'He says he can't do anything about it,' Ariana translated. 'He thinks the Buggy must be very tired. These people reason in terms of a donkey: they don't understand about engines!'

The dark little man repeated his apologies and drove away, his splendid moustache drooping a little because of his lamentable inability to assist them in their hour of need.

'What do we do now?' Rhea asked.

'Wait.' Ariana looked hopeful again. 'Someone is sure to come along—someone who knows about engines.'

It was another ten minutes before they heard the approaching car as it came smoothly up the hill behind them, and when it finally rounded the bend on the road there was no doubt about the man who had come to their rescue. Nicolas Metaxas sprang from the grey convertible as soon as it came to a halt just ahead of them.

'Oh, *Nicos*, I thought you would be miles away by now!' Ariana cried, running towards him. 'We've broken down.'

'So it would seem,' he remarked grimly. 'Are you all right otherwise?'

He was looking directly at Rhea, his blue eyes genuinely concerned.

'Perfectly,' she assured him. 'We've been unlucky, that's all. Neither of us knows a great deal about cars.'

'I've never been completely stranded before,' Ariana said plaintively. 'There's always been someone around, but this time there was nobody passing except an old farmer with a donkey-cart who knew less about engines than we do. But now you are here all is well!' She heaved a deep sigh of relief. 'I thought you would have been much ahead of us and over on Euboea by now.'

'I had a call to make at Marathon,' he explained, moving towards the stranded Renault. 'It seems it was just as well!'

'Someone would have come,' Ariana repeated ungraciously. 'Oh, I'm sorry!' she apologised immediately. 'I didn't mean we are not much in your debt, Nicolas, but you know how busy this road generally is——'

He was already inspecting the engine, his head under the bonnet, so perhaps he did not hear. It was several minutes before he spoke again.

'I can't do anything with it,' he confessed. 'It will have to be taken to the nearest garage.' He closed the bonnet with a decisive snap, turning to them where they stood on the road. 'It seems we're back at A again,' he observed with the faintest of smiles. 'Get in!'

They crossed to the convertible while he rescued Rhea's suitcases from the Renault's boot, collecting Ariana's personal belongings and her car-keys from the driver's seat.

'Will it be all right?' Ariana was loath to leave her beloved Renault. 'It could be broken into.'

'We're almost at the bridge, and I'll have it collected as soon as we get across.' Nicolas opened the passenger door of the convertible. 'We can all sit in front, I think.'

The back seat was packed with boxes of various sizes and shapes, on top of which stood a milliner's hat-box striped in silver and mauve and a lady's umbrella.

'You've been buying presents for your mother!' Ariana observed. 'How is she, Nicolas? We haven't seen her for some time.'

'She is well,' he said, smiling faintly and without confirming her supposition about either the hat-box or the umbrella. 'Perhaps you will find time to visit her one of these days, or I may bring her to Volponé.'

'That would please Grandmama very much,' Ariana declared, stepping aside to let Rhea into the convertible. 'You will have a better view if you sit in the middle,' she advised.

The remainder of their journey sped past very quickly, and all the way to Volponé Rhea was acutely aware of the man sitting so close beside her in the front of the car. Once or twice, when she tore her eyes away from the magnificent panorama of sky and sea and mountains to look at him, he turned his head briefly to offer her an explanation or make some reference to their destination, but it was Ariana who kept up a barrage of conversation as they sped along. Nicolas Metaxas seemed to be thinking deeply about something else.

Presently they were going down a steep, winding road through rock cuttings to where the strait ahead of them had contracted to a narrow channel and from their superb viewpoint they could see a gleaming white town on the farther side. Dazzled in the sunlight, Rhea picked out the truncated polygonal minaret of a mosque and the pointed arches of a basilica, while rising sheer behind them a tree-clad mountain peak stood out against the cloudless blue of the Aegean sky. She drew in a swift breath, unable to express her appreciation and wonder, and once again her father's memory came very near. The man beside her did not speak, as if he had guessed that her thoughts were busy with the past and were not to be disturbed.

Once they crossed the bridge he pulled up at a garage where he gave his instructions about the stranded Renault, and then they were through Khalkiss and motoring swiftly along the north shore of the Euripos with the mountains ahead of them shadowed by the westering sun.

The rugged mountains of Greece were a revelation to Rhea and the deeply-indented coastline with its white-sanded bays was a wonderful surprise. Every turn of the road revealed its sheltered inlet where deep blue water lapped the shore and the strong current of the channel poured out to meet the sea.

When they finally turned northwards the mountains were behind them, sheltering them from the wind.

'We're nearly there now,' Ariana said, sitting forward in her seat as if coming home would always be an event for her. 'We have made up all our lost time, thanks to Nicolas!'

Abruptly Nicolas turned the car towards the mountains again and they began to climb through a parched landscape to the crest of a long ridge where a few sparse Aleppo pines stood out darkly against the lighter scree. It looked wild and desolate, and Rhea felt disappointment flowing through her like a dark tide.

'We are not there yet,' Nicolas said with a faint smile as if he had guessed her mood. 'This is only our frontier, the barrier that keeps the winds at bay.'

Once over the summit the picture changed dramatically. Before them a wide, deep valley lay peacefully in the sun with Alpine meadows shining on its sides and terrace after terrace of vines stepping down to the silver thread of a river winding its way through a narrow gorge crowned by a tower. Hill after hill rolled away to higher mountains on the horizon, pale now against the paling sky, and soon they were driving between fields of rich loam where the crops were already high and a row of poplars cast their stiff shadows on the road to Volponé.

'Everybody will be waiting!' Ariana exclaimed. 'But they will be surprised that it is Nicolas who has brought us home.'

The final word struck a deep chord in Rhea's heart as she remembered her father who had tried over many years to provide a home for her in England and how anxious he had been to secure her happiness as a child. He must have come here as a young man to her mother's home in this deep and lovely valley among the mountains before he had carried Maria Karousis off as a bride to his own land.

Everything in the hidden valley lay still in the afternoon heat as they passed through a tiny village where the inevitable group of men sat smoking and talking under a convenient plane tree outside the one *taverna* in the dusty square. Ariana waved to them as she passed, and Rhea was carefully inspected as she sat by Nicolas Metaxas's side in the open car.

'They will know all about you by now,' Ariana said. 'Someone will have arrived from Volponé with the lastest news.'

They began to climb again, winding up a narrow lane past a church to leave the village behind, and then, suddenly, there it was.

Volponé lay in full sunshine, a squat white stucco farmhouse with a paved courtyard before it where a single plane tree in the centre afforded the only shade. Bushes of bright orange oleanders blazed on either side of the house, vying with the muted red of the old roof tiles and the scarlet glory of geraniums just in flower.

At the sound of their approach the door of the house opened to reveal a tall woman in a severely-tailored black dress, her thick black hair pulled back into a knot behind her head. Her face had no semblance of beauty about it and her eyes were hard.

'Rhea,' Ariana announced as she got down from the car, 'this is Aunt Evadne, Daphne's mother.'

Evadne Capodistrias inclined her head in acknowledgement, although Rhea felt that it was no more than a token gesture to conventionality on her aunt's part.

'You will be made welcome,' Evadne said in stilted English. 'My mother is ready to meet you.'

Rhea turned back towards the car where Nicolas Metaxas was lifting her suitcases from the boot.

'Thank you for getting me here in one piece,' she said. 'I'm sure Ariana's Buggy would never have made it!'

He straightened as her aunt moved away from the open door.

'Don't let Evadne intimidate you,' he advised unexpectedly. 'She is embittered by her widowhood and her sense of obligation in the house, and she never had a son. Her husband was wounded in the war and was an added burden to her for many years; he died not long after Daphne was born. Evadne will not welcome you as the others will.'

For a moment Rhea felt acutely disconcerted by this unexpected warning of hostility on the part of her aunt, especially as it came from Nicolas, who appeared to be Daphne's constant companion when she was in Greece.

'I'd rather find out these things for myself,' she said

almost dismissively. 'After all, we're family and that should make a difference.'

'It's the one thing that won't influence your aunt,' he answered slowly. 'Family means Greek to her—nothing else.'

Rhea followed Evadne Capodistrias into the house, leaving Ariana to deal with Nicolas, to invite him to stay or see him on his way, whichever she considered politic in the circumstances.

Her aunt led the way across a shadowy hall, over a checkered floor of black and white tiles worn by the tread of generations into shallow undulations, until they came to a stout door on its far side which stood ajar.

'In here,' she directed almost sullenly.

The room they entered was full of light filtering in through open patio doors which led to the garden where a table had been set under a vine pergola. Geraniums and petunias in large terracotta pots stood at intervals around the ancient stone terrace, while narrow marble benches flanked each side of a pathway leading to an orchard behind the farmhouse itself. A faint, indefinable scent drifted towards her from the far side of the pergola as she walked forward, unable to put a name to it at first.

'My mother is waiting,' Evadne said.

They crossed the terrace to another door where a small woman in black was standing under the lintel. She was so like Ariana that there could be no mistaking her identity.

'Grandmama!' Rhea said.

She walked forward to kiss the parched cheek, finding both her hands clasped in thin, strong fingers as Phaedra Karousis looked steadily back at her.

'Maria's girl,' she said with faint reserve. 'You are welcome to Volponé.'

Quick tears gathered in Rhea's eyes as she realised what a tremendous effort her grandmother had made to welcome her in her own language, prompted, no doubt by Ariana, who had learned English at school. It would be difficult for them to communicate, she knew, but perhaps the pressure of a hand or an answering smile would work wonders where words were difficult to come by.

'She won't understand everything you say,' Evadne pointed out, 'but she has sharp eyes. You will not be able to impress her easily.'

'If we are both our natural selves I think that will be enough,' Rhea answered quietly. 'Will you explain for me that I am sorry to be late?'

Evadne spoke in Greek for the first time while her mother moved away in the direction of the orchard.

'She wishes you to meet your grandfather now,' Evadne turned to say in English. 'He spends much of his time in the garden.'

Moving in single file, they re-crossed the terrace to walk out under the vine pergola towards the orchard and, once again Rhea was conscious of the sharp, pungent scent which had assailed her nostrils when she had first arrived. Bitter-sweet and almost cloying, it hung in the air like something tangible, yet it had a sharpness about it which she seemed to recognise. It was stronger than the perfume of roses and more insidious than the scent of the stocks along the borders, but there was no sign of any other flower as the path ended in a small arbour where an old man sat in the shade.

He was older than she had expected, Rhea thought as they looked at each other for the first time, grey eyes questioning brown in that initial moment of recognition, as if John Karousis was every bit as uncertain of her acceptance of him as she was of his. Then the brown eyes cleared and the wrinkled cheeks were further creased in an expansive smile.

'Welcome to Volponé!' he said. 'You are like your father, my child.'

It was something she had not expected to hear; a recognition of the man from England who had spirited away his younger daughter, carrying her off to his distant homeland never to return.

'Grandpapa!' Rhea buried her face in his flowing white beard, kissing the wrinkled cheek above it. 'I'm so glad I came!'

She helped him to his feet.

'It has been a long time,' he said in halting English. 'A very long time. But you will stay here and get to know us and that will be good.'

Evadne was standing close behind them, her sharply-indrawn breath audible in the silence.

'I have a meal ready,' she announced bleakly, 'and Nicolas Metaxas is here.'

'He brought us in his car when we broke down on the mainland side of the bridge,' Rhea explained. 'It was very kind of him.'

The old man's smile broadened.

'He is for ever getting Ariana out of trouble,' he acknowledged. 'What was it this time?'

'The engine, I think. He is having it taken to a garage to be put right,' Rhea explained, 'but he promised it would be delivered here in the morning.'

'Nicolas gets things done,' her grandfather chuckled. 'He has not gone away?'

'He is with Ariana,' Evadne said quickly. 'I will go and ask him to eat with us.'

Ariana came rushing in to embrace her grandfather who held her at arm's length to look at her.

'What is this?' he demanded playfully. 'You promised me that you would get to the airport and back without trouble, and now you have no car!'

'I will have one again tomorrow,' Ariana assured him. 'Nicolas has promised.'

Nicolas Metaxas was standing on the terrace when they moved in from the orchard and there was no doubt about the quality of the friendship which existed between the two men in spite of the difference in their ages.

'You have stayed away too long, Nicos,' the older man admonished. 'I have missed your conversation very much.'

'I have a lot to tell you,' Nicolas assured him as they shook hands. 'I have been in Turkey and Egypt and once again in Rome.'

'You are never still,' the old man said. 'Never without somewhere to go!'

'That's business these days.' Nicolas sat down on one of the marble benches beside him. 'I'd like to talk to you about your wine. I have already a market for it, if you will agree to sell at the price.'

Ariana led Rhea away.

'They'll argue there till it's time to eat,' she declared. 'Men are always talking about business! Come, and I will show you to your room.'

They ascended a shallow staircase between white-washed walls with small alcoves at intervals where a deeply-recessed window let in the light, passing one stout door after another in the corridor above till they came to one which stood invitingly open.

'Here you are!' Ariana said. 'Yianni has already delivered your suitcases and the bathroom is in there. We will share it because my room is next to yours.'

The bedroom she entered delighted Rhea, because it was so essentially Greek with an atmosphere which reflected a certain practicality without appearing to be cold, and the small posy of flowers on the window sill had been carefully arranged as an extra welcoming touch, probably by her cousin. Shutters covered by net curtains shaded the room from the fiercer heat of the noonday sun and the beautiful wooden floor glowed with the rich patina of age. Two hand-woven rugs flanked the single bed with its heavy wooden headboard, and a lovely old table in a corner held candlesticks and a decorated water-jug and glass. Next to the window a carved chest-of-drawers was to serve her as a dressing table and a second door led into the bathroom she was to share with her cousin.

'It used to be a dressing-room,' Ariana explained. 'Come down when you are ready and I will help you to unpack later. It is as well not to keep Aunt Evadne waiting too long when she has prepared a meal.'

Glad to be able to wash in cool spring water and change out of her soiled travelling clothes, Rhea put on the pink linen dress she had placed carefully on top of her smaller suitcase, brushing her hair vigorously to shake out the dust after their ride in the open convertible. It had been a glorious way to complete the second half of her remarkable journey, she thought, with the fresh wind blowing in from the sea and the warm sun on her face. She had certainly enjoyed it and their adventure with the recalcitrant little Buggy had turned out better than she had expected.

On her way to the door she paused for a moment beside the open window, realising that her room was situated at the front of the house, overlooking the gravelled terrace and facing a narrow valley and the distant sea. The sun had gone from this side of Volponé, leaving it in shadow, but an orange-gold light bathed the hillside opposite, turning the sky above it to a deep vermilion and lying gently on a grove of trees. An olive grove! As far as she could see the sturdy little trees marched in their serried ranks up the hillside to where they met the vines, but it was the scent of lemon blossom wafted towards her in the still air which she finally recognised and knew she would never forget. It had been her first impression of Volponé, where her mother had been born.

Footsteps crunched across the gravel beneath her balcony and she let the lace curtain fall into place as Nicolas Metaxas and her grandfather walked towards the olive grove, deep in conversation. They were two of a kind, she decided, responsive to the needs of their land and the wellbeing of their respective families, and they had long been friends. The old man appeared to respect Nicolas's opinion and Nicolas probably sought to gain from her grandfather's long experience.

When they turned back towards the house Ariana came running towards them, flinging her arms impulsively about Nicolas's neck. This was followed by a spate of rapid Greek to which he listened intently until her cousin's impulsive little greeting was over.

Kissing him on both cheeks, Ariana stood back for a moment to look at him, the strange red light in the western sky reflected on her face and in her glowing eyes, and suddenly Rhea was aware of an almost unbearable tension as she watched. Then Nicolas flung back his head and laughed, kissing her in return as John

Karousis beamed at them both. Nicolas turned then, walking with them back to the house, and suddenly he was looking directly up at the window, but surely he could not see her standing there, watching!

CHAPTER TWO

THE meal which Evadne set before them was typically Greek, starting with a rich chicken broth, thickened with rice and eggs and flavoured with lemon, and ending with a yellow-fleshed melon which Rhea found delightful. Generous portions of shellfish had been handed round in between with a simple sauce of oil and lemon, followed by a large pot containing a mouth-watering ragout which her aunt brought to the table with considerable pride.

It was cool on the patio now that the sun had gone down, but they lingered for a long time over their first meal together—a family meal, Rhea thought with a contented smile. When the lamps were lit and hung, like huge fireflies, along the edge of the vine pergola they lingered over their sweet Turkish coffee and preserved fruit till it was time to say good night. It was eleven o'clock, but the light was still strong with the first stars showing palely through and a crescent moon, like a pale silver sickle, hanging low in the eastern sky.

Ariana popped a last piece of Turkish delight into her mouth as they moved towards the stairs.

'Are you too tired to talk?' she asked.

'Not in the least,' Rhea declared, 'but we might disturb the others.'

'Only Aunt Evadne sleeps on our side of the house and she will be too tired to lie awake listening to our chatter,' her cousin decided. 'Besides, I promised to help you unpack. Do let me help you, Rhea,' she pleaded, 'because I think we are more like sisters than cousins. Daphne is so different,' she added slowly, 'not really one of us, though she is Greek. She has such different ideas, though I suppose she *is* family. It's most important in Greece, you see—being "family", I mean. We are so contented to be together, and I think that is why Nicolas comes back to Florina so often. His mother will not part with their home, even when he is so often away from it on business. He is a good son, you see.'

Once again Rhea found herself wondering about her young cousin's affection for Nicolas Metaxas; but surely Ariana's attitude was too free to go hand-in-hand with a hidden love?

'Our two families have always been close,' Ariana explained. 'There was only one thing——' She paused, looking at Rhea as if she might offer an apology before she ran on in her usual informative way, 'My grandmother still thinks Nicolas should have been her grandson, because your mother was engaged to his father when she met *your* father.'

'And married him,' Rhea reflected aloud. 'They were in love and that mattered a lot.'

'Oh, yes,' said Ariana. 'It is all that matters.'

She was a true romantic, steeped in the legendary love affairs of her race. Looking daily towards Mount Olympus where the gods had loved and plotted, quarrelled and avenged themselves in the most spectacular ways, how could she be otherwise? Shining Apollo and Heracles and Achilles were still her heroes, and deep in her heart she was Aphrodite rising naked from the waves.

As she opened the smaller of her two suitcases Rhea wondered if her grandmother still resented that old love affair which had taken a beloved younger daughter away from Greece. It could be the reason for the suggestion of reserve that had stood for a moment between them when they first met, although she had attributed it to their lack of a common language. Certainly it hadn't inhibited her grandfather in any way. John Karousis had been entirely natural, welcoming her with open arms.

Ariana opened the cupboard which stood against the wall, bringing coathangers for her clothes.

'Aunt Evadne makes them in her spare time,' she explained, holding one up for her cousin's inspection. 'They are rather pretty, don't you think?'

'They're lovely,' Rhea said. 'Such beautiful handwork. She must be a very busy person.'

Ariana shrugged. 'She goes nowhere, so she has plenty of time for her needlework, and Nicolas's mother sells them for her in Athens.'

Nicolas Metaxas's name seemed to crop up everywhere, Rhea thought, dominating their lives in its own way. She had even been dramatically aware of him before she had known who he was, meeting that compelling gaze as soon as she had set foot on Greek soil at the airport. She lifted a thin cotton dress, shaking it out almost angrily.

'Oh!' Ariana exclaimed. 'How lovely!'

She was looking at the necklet which Rhea had placed on the chest-of-drawers in case she might decide to wear it.

'It is lovely,' Rhea agreed. 'It was a gift from my father shortly before he died in a car crash in America, and it has always meant Greece to me.'

'You know what it is, of course?' Ariana asked. 'It's an ancient torque such as is often found at a "dig", and it could be valuable.'

Rhea picked up the necklet.

'It's only a copy of the real thing,' she said, handing it over for her cousin's inspection.

'It's a very good copy, in that case,' Ariana declared. 'Have you worn it much in England?'

'Not very often,' Rhea answered. 'It's very heavy and—it didn't seem to belong there.'

'Will you wear it now?' her cousin asked curiously. 'It is a love token, you know.'

'And I have no right to wear it until—someone I love gives it to me?' Rhea asked. 'But my father and I were very close.'

'That is not the same,' Ariana told her. 'You will see!'

She put the necklet down on the dressing-chest where Rhea had already laid our her hairbrush and comb, still looking at it with appraising eyes.

'You must show it to Nicolas,' she suggested. 'He has a great interest in these things, although he is not an archaeologist by profession, like his father. Kyrie Metaxas was very rich, you understand, and he bought a remote island—one of the Cyclades—very small, you understand, but he started a "dig" there and found several artefacts.'

'My father worked with him for a short time,' Rhea remembered. 'It was how he met my mother.'

'Yes, I know.' Ariana bit her lip. 'It was many years ago.'

Rhea closed the lid of her empty suitcase.

'Ariana,' she asked, 'did Kyrie Metaxas sell the island—afterwards?'

Her cousin shook her head.

'Oh, no. It's still in the family. Nicolas goes there quite often to sail his boat, and now he has opened up the original excavations in the hope of finding more artefacts for the small museum he is building there. It isn't big, you understand; just in keeping with the island, and so far there isn't much of importance. A few ikons have been found, and a lot of pottery. Also there has been some Byzantine stoneware and pieces of jewellery, like your torque, although nothing is intact.' She turned to look at the necklet again. 'It is quite unique,' she decided.

'The original will be in the museum, I suppose,' Rhea suggested.

Ariana shook her head.

'Alas,' she said, 'it was stolen. Kyrie Metaxas was very distressed about it disappearing, but it was never found in his lifetime. Kyrie Metaxas calls it "that old torque", but Nicolas would like to recover it, I'm sure. You see, he thinks it belongs on Norbos, where it was found.' She paused on her way to the door. 'He could have a copy of it, like yours,' she mused, 'but it wouldn't be the same. He would not put a fake in his museum, you understand.'

'Of course not,' Rhea agreed. 'That would be—sort of cheating.'

'Nicolas would never cheat,' her cousin said with conviction. 'He believes in himself.' She paused to look back at her cousin from England. 'Have you ever been on a dig, Rhea?' she asked.

'To my shame—never,' Rhea confessed. 'I was too

busy being "educated" in other matters in England and my father hadn't a lot of time to indulge his hobby once he left Greece. He had a successful business career, like Nicolas,' she added almost drily.

'It is lucky for Nicolas that he can combine the two,' her cousin said thoughtfully. 'Often we go to Norbos to help him, and it's fun as well as being interesting. Would you like to go one day?'

Rhea stood quite still in the centre of the room. Could she go to Norbos? Could she set foot on the island where it all began—the loving and the heartache which had separated two friends and given her a mother from this strange and lovely country where she felt at home?

'I don't know,' she heard herself answering. 'It would all depend on Nicolas—whether he would want that or not.'

'*Everybody* is welcome to go,' Ariana assured her. 'Everyone Nicolas can trust, you understand. You must be really caring on a dig or you could cause much damage to the artefacts you might discover. It needs patience, but I think you have plenty of patience,' she decided.

'Does Daphne help?' Rhea found herself asking for no very definite reason.

The question made her cousin laugh.

'Daphne? Good gracious, no! She has lovely hands to keep without a flaw, so she would not risk digging, even with gloves on, but she goes to the island quite often to relax in the sunshine and swim in the sea, which she considers good for her figure. The dig isn't what she goes to Norbos for, you understand. She is the most beautiful one, and most cruel. In many ways she is like her mother, although Aunt Evadne is not beautiful.'

A clock struck somewhere in the quiet house as she opened the bedroom door.

'It's midnight,' Rhea said, 'we've been gossiping for over an hour!'

Ariana came back to kiss her on the cheek.

'I really love you,' she said. 'We are going to be good friends.'

When her cousin had gone Rhea crossed to the open window to look out for a moment before she went to bed for the first time in the old, white-walled farmhouse that had been her mother's childhood home, seeing the myriad stars in the vast firmament above her head and listening to the little sounds of the night as she thought how happy she would be to live here for ever. She realised that the reality could only last for a little while, however. She was not here to stay.

Between her and the vision of the gentle Athenian night a man's luminous eyes dominated all the other impressions of her long, eventful day; but perhaps Nicolas Metaxas expected that if he was so accustomed to conquest. Perhaps he was the eternal lover, like all-powerful Zeus who wrought so much havoc on Olympus long ago.

Turning away from the window, she saw the necklet lying on the chest beside her bed and the yellow stones seemed to dominate all the others as she looked. What had she called them? 'Evil eyes'. But that was quite ridiculous! They were, like the others, just clever imitations of the real things.

She woke the following morning to a strong light streaming in through her shutters and when she flung them back she saw the whole, long valley aglow under the early morning sun. As far as the eyes could see the rolling foothills stretched away to an amphitheatre of mountains clothed with pines, while nearer at hand, on this eastern side of the house, a long grove of olive trees basked in the amazing light.

'It's something essentially Greek,' Ariana said from the doorway. 'You will not see it anywhere else, and when you go to the islands you will find it dominating everything else. I think that is what makes our ancient buildings look so dramatic,' she added thoughtfully. 'The light on pale marble and the final setting of the sun.'

Rhea turned to her eagerly.

'I love Greece, Ariana,' she said, 'and I'm already captivated. I know there must be so much to see, and you will show it to me.'

'Get dressed and I will show you the garden first,' her cousin commanded. 'It is going to be very warm by midday, so it's best to walk early in the morning when it is cool.'

'You have had your breakfast,' Rhea guessed, ashamed that she had slept so long and so soundly that she had failed to hear the first stirring of the household or even the crowing of a cock in the adjacent farm.

'We rise very early,' Ariana agreed, 'but you had a long journey from London yesterday and must have felt tired.'

'I'll apologise to Aunt Evadne,' Rhea promised, 'and it won't happen again. I'd like to help in the house, Ariana,' she added spontaneously. 'There must be something I can do.'

Her cousin shrugged her shoulders.

'We all have our tasks,' she agreed, 'but Evadne must make the decision. She is the—housekeeper, don't you say?'

Rhea nodded.

'I'll follow you down,' she said.

When she reached the kitchen her aunt was already supervising the cooking of their evening meal.

'I've slept late this morning, Aunt Evadne,' she apologised quickly, 'but it won't happen again. I like to be up and about in the early morning, and it's even more lovely here than I expected.' She crossed to the open door which led on to the end of the terrace. 'Have I kept you waiting?'

'Your breakfast is set for you outside,' she was informed ungraciously. 'It is warm enough now to sit in the sun.' Her aunt took a coffee pot from a large stove in the corner, waiting to follow her out. 'If there is anything else you need you will let me know.'

Chilled by the unfriendly tone, Rhea took her seat at the wrought iron table under a cascading wisteria where a plate, cup and saucer had been left as the only evidence of the family breakfast long since finished.

'I don't mean to be a nuisance,' she said, 'or to cause unnecessary work. Please let me help in the house, Aunt Evadne. I'd really appreciate that.'

Coming back to the table with a jug of orange juice and a plate of warm croissants covered by a napkin, Evadne paused behind her chair.

'There is no need for you to help with the housework,' she declared firmly. 'I have a woman in the kitchen to help with the cooking and a girl to clean upstairs. That is as much help as we need in the ordinary way. Ariana, of course, is expected to look after her own room and sometimes wait at the table.'

'Then, let me do the same,' Rhea suggested. 'I am accustomed to looking after myself and I could help Ariana.'

Her aunt poured her coffee for her with pointed deliberation, setting down the ornate Turkish pot at her elbow.

'That is not necessary,' she returned coldly. 'We never allow a guest to work in the house.'

Rhea felt as if a douche of cold water had been flung in her face.

'But surely it is not the same,' she protested. 'I—hardly think of myself as a guest.' Her eyes clouded a little. 'I thought I might become one of the family.'

'That is impossible,' Evadne returned harshly. 'You are not Greek.'

'My mother was,' Rhea pointed out. 'I thought—perhaps that would make a difference.'

'It makes much difference. She left Volponé to go to London,' her aunt reminded her.

'Only because she fell in love,' Rhea protested. 'She left because she married my father and went to make a home for him.'

'In a country that was not her own.' Evadne emphasised the point. 'She could never have been happy in London, and she died very soon afterwards.'

'Yes,' Rhea agreed with deep regret, 'but I know she was happy while she lived there. We talked of her often when I was old enough to understand, and my father never married again.'

Evadne made her way towards the kitchen.

'He was a man of much determination,' she said, 'and he took her away from Greece. You will never convince

me that my sister was truly happy in your country,
however much you try.'

Rhea set her orange juice aside, feeling that she had
no heart for her breakfast now.

'Aren't you going to eat the croissants?' Ariana
enquired, appearing at the end of the vine pergola.
'They are delicious, especially with the cherry jam we
make in the autumn. The honey is our own, too,' she
added, 'and it is also very good.'

Rhea had been aware of the drone of bees ever since
she had come on to the terrace, and she watched them
hovering among the flowers for a moment before she
spoke.

'I can't just sit around doing nothing, Ariana, but it
appears I can't help in the house. I've just asked Aunt
Evadne what I could do and the answer was—nothing.
Surely she must know how I feel.'

Ariana sat down beside her, pouring herself a cup of
coffee.

'She only knows how Evadne feels,' she declared with
amazing insight. 'She is a very bitter person who has a
deep grudge towards fate because her husband died
before she could have a son.'

'She has Daphne,' Rhea pointed out.

'That is not the same.' Her cousin turned from the
table as a large Persian cat stalked across the terrace,
eyeing Rhea with wide, baleful eyes. 'This is Artemis,'
she introduced the feline invader. 'She will not accept
you immediately, but you can win her round.'

'Do you think I will ever be able to win round Aunt
Evadne?' Rhea asked, ignoring the cat. 'That seems to
be more important.'

'You can try.' Ariana put a saucer full of milk on the
polished slabs of the terrace for the cat. 'It isn't easy to
impress people right away. Artemis likes to stand on
her dignity for a while, for instance, and there are some
people she will never like. One of them is Nicolas,' she
added with a little laugh.

'Why do you think that is?' Rhea enquired.

'Because Nicolas has always teased her. Even when she
was a quite small kitten Artemis didn't like to be teased.'

'Have you heard anything from Nicolas about your car?' Rhea asked, steering the conversation away from irascible felines who wanted to stand on their dignity. 'He said he would let you know as soon as possible.'

'He hasn't telephoned,' Ariana admitted. 'He may have been too busy.'

It was a feasible enough excuse, but Ariana was evidently disappointed.

'When you are ready,' she said, 'we will walk down through the olive grove.'

'I'm ready now.' Rhea got to her feet. 'Should I take a hat? The sun looks very bright.'

'Oh, no,' Ariana said, 'it doesn't get really hot for an hour yet and we'll be walking under the trees.'

'I must say good morning to Grandpapa,' Rhea decided. 'Where will he be?'

'Smoking his pipe on the terrace under your bedroom window,' Ariana said. 'He likes the east side of the house in the morning when the sun is on it. Grandmama won't be downstairs yet,' she added. 'She tidies up for both of them.'

John Karousis was standing on the edge of the gravel terrace looking down towards the olive grove when Rhea found him and he turned towards her eagerly, holding out both hands as she approached.

'Kaliméra!' he greeted her with a beaming smile. 'You have come to look more closely at my view,' he added, kissing her on both cheeks. 'Alas! the blossom is gone from most of the trees, but you can still smell its scent and the scent of lemon. The bees love it and come every morning while there is still one tiny spray of blossom left. They also come for the honeysuckle, which is everywhere around.'

'I can smell it,' Rhea said, drawing in a deep breath of the perfumed air. 'How far are we from the sea?'

'Not very far,' he said, drawing reflectively on his pipe, 'but it is a rocky coast and you must be careful. Many boats have been wrecked on our shores; many men have lost their lives sailing back from the Islands.' He watched her as she looked across the olive grove.

'Are you going to be happy here, my granddaughter?' he asked. 'Are you going to stay?'

A strange little sigh caught in Rhea's throat.

'If I only could,' she said. 'But one day I will have to go.'

'Back to London?' he asked. 'Perhaps you have someone waiting there for you, as Nicolas suggested.'

She did not know they had discussed her in such a personal way and she wondered why.

'I have no one,' she answered.

'No one to be in love with?' His tone was teasing. 'Surely that can not be possible?'

'Once—there was someone,' she confessed, 'but that is over now. It was a long time ago, and he married someone else.'

She found it easy to confide in this man whom she had known for so short a time. Warm-hearted and generous, he was her especial favourite and she felt that he would never try to fob her off with evasion if she should ask an awkward question as the rest of the family might—Grandmama because of her deep-rooted sense of family pride; Aunt Evadne because of her aversion to all things foreign, and Ariana because she would never hurt anyone if she could substitute a half-truth which would be less unkind. Ariana loved the whole world, and especially Artemis of the baleful yellow eyes, who resented Nicolas because she did not like to be teased.

'Ariana and I are going for a short walk,' she told the old man. 'She wants to show me the orchard.'

'Don't go too far,' he warned. 'The sun will soon be very hot. Has her car arrived from the garage yet?'

'Not so far,' Rhea said. 'It's still early.'

'She spoke of taking you for a short tour on the mainland, but it's best to travel early in the day. Perhaps,' he added optimistically, 'her car will be returned soon, as Nicolas promised.'

Ariana came to stand beside them.

'No sign of Nicolas or the car,' she sighed. 'Perhaps it will be here when we return.' She kissed her grandfather on either cheek. 'Where do you go today?'

'To look at some timber Nicolas wishes to buy from us,' he answered, pleased by her interest. 'We will start to thin out the forest in the autumn when the grape harvest is in.'

'You do not wish to lose your trees,' Ariana said.

He looked beyond the olive grove to the vista of tree-clad hills and the mountains beyond them.

'There are many trees,' he said, 'and one day we will plant again. The years pass and we all have a task to do for the land.'

'He must regret the fact that he has no son to follow him at Volponé—not even a son-in-law,' Ariana mused as they left John Karousis to his contemplation of the future. 'Yet he does not say so because he accepts life as it is. He has not become bitter, as Evadne has, thinking always of the past and what could have been if things had been different. If Greece had not been decimated by so many wars and revolutions in the past, for instance. He sees Volponé as his personal trust, but that is all.'

They walked down into the olive grove, wandering between the rows of trees where the hum of bees drowned every other sound until they came to a barrier of rock rising to a higher plain.

'This is as far as we go,' Ariana said. 'It is the boundary of our land. Up there on the plateau among the mountains is Florina, where Nicolas lives with his mother, although neither of them are there very often. Like Daphne, Kyria Metaxas has a flat in Athens and she comes to Florina only at the ending of the week.'

'Nicolas seemed to be very fond of his home,' Rhea suggested.

'Oh, he is! It is just that they both have to be away a lot. Perhaps one day he will marry and settle down at Florina to grow more trees,' Ariana suggested. 'Already he has planted many and would wish to purchase more land, but that is not so easy in Greece nowadays.' She led the way up a narrow path which climbed to the plateau. 'There!' she said when they had reached the top. 'You can see Florina now.'

Looking down a long valley between rolling foothills

she pointed to a white house in the distance perched on a plateau of its own.

'Florina is a very beautiful place,' she added almost wistfully. 'I wonder if our cousin Daphne will go there one day.'

'As Nicolas's wife?' Rhea asked stiffly.

'That is what I meant,' Ariana said, 'though I would not wish it.'

Rhea turned to look at her.

'Why, Ariana?' she asked.

'Because she is not the one for him.' The reply was unequivocal in the extreme. 'I told you she was cruel, did I not? She is also calculating. It is always what is best for Daphne which occupies her mind and I do not consider that is good enough for Nicolas.'

'It may be what he wants,' Rhea pointed out. 'Daphne, I mean. He could be genuinely in love with her.'

'That is true,' her cousin allowed regretfully. 'It would also be a good match for Daphne in her mother's eyes.' She laughed suddenly as they turned back down the path. 'What a curious family you must think us,' she declared, 'Always prying into each other's affairs, but it is the way in Greece. We have great interest in every member of the family and like to know what is going on. That is why Grandpapa wanted to send for you as soon as we knew your other grandparants had died.'

Walking back through the olive grove Rhea thought how wonderful it would be to stay at Volponé for a very long time.

When they finally reached the house they could hear voices on the terrace under the vine pergola.

'It's Nicolas!' Ariana exclaimed, hurrying forward. 'He must have come with my car.'

Nicolas Metaxas rose to his feet as they approached, the smile Rhea remembered so vividly creasing the corners of his eyes.

'*Kaliméra!*' he saluted them. 'I thought I would find you still asleep!'

'Because of yesterday?' Ariana challenged. 'Well, that

is not so. We have been for a long walk right to the end
of the olive grove and up to the plateau by the little
path. That is a considerable way, you will surely agree,
Nicos, but have you brought my car? I wished to take
Rhea to Larisa across the ferry and up to Olympus,
perhaps.'

The smile faded from his eyes.

'I'm sorry about the car,' he apologised, including
Rhea in his explanation, 'but it is to be a longer job
than I expected.' He glanced briefly in John Karousis's
direction, as if they had already discussed the matter in
some detail. 'It will be best to have it overhauled
completely, and perhaps given a new coat of paint.'

'But what are we to do without it?' Ariana wailed.
'We will be able to go nowhere!'

'That is an exaggeration,' Nicolas pointed out calmly.
'It will be no more than three days before it is returned
to you in a safe condition—far safer than before,' he
added carefully.

'It has never let me down completely,' Ariana
protested from the depth of her disappointment.

'It did yesterday,' Nicolas reminded her, smiling
faintly. 'It is not the end of the world, and I will come
to your rescue again, if you will let me,' he added.
'Tomorrow I will be going to Agrinion on business and
I can offer you a lift to Delphi, where you can consult
the Oracle, if you like,' he suggested, tongue in cheek.
'It is not out of my way and you can browse among the
ruins till I return.'

'Why are you going to Agrinion?' asked Ariana, half-
placated by his offer to drive them there.

'To buy timber, as usual,' he told her, again glancing
in Rhea's direction. 'Will you come?'

'Of course we will come!' answered Ariana immediately. 'Rhea must see *everything*!'

'A tall order, indeed!' Nicolas smiled. 'I'll call for you
early—about eight o'clock—if you can be ready by
then.'

'It is no trouble,' Ariana assured him. 'I am often out
of bed by seven, especially in the summer when the
birds won't let you sleep. We will prepare a picnic,' she

offered. 'It is nice to eat outside, especially in the mountains on a sunny day. Nicos,' she added before anyone else could draw breath, 'will it be permissible to use your swimming-pool one afternoon while Rhea is with us? Last year I have used it often without disturbing anyone, and we will not make a nuisance of ourselves if you agree.'

'For someone so small, you make a large and roundabout speech!' he teased, putting an arm round her shoulders. 'Of course you can use the pool. I was about to suggest it, as a matter of fact, to mitigate your disappointment about the Buggy, and Rhea ought to see Florina at its best—in the spring.'

Wondering what his mother would have to say about such an arrangement, Rhea was pleased enough at the prospect of a swim at any time of the day.

'You're being very kind,' she told him, 'but I wouldn't want to intrude in any way.'

He looked at her directly.

'If you were likely to intrude I wouldn't have made the suggestion,' he said lightly. 'Florina is too seldom used; a house needs to be lived in to make it a home. One day I hope to have more time to live there myself,' he mused, 'but first of all I must earn some money to keep it as it is.'

'It looked very beautiful,' she was forced to acknowledge. 'We saw it from the edge of the escarpment above the olive grove. Is it very old?'

'About two hundred years. In that time my family has planted many trees, and felled them, too, and we were lucky to escape the devastation of wars. When you go to Florina you will probably understand,' he added before he turned to her grandfather to continue the conversation their arrival had interrupted a few minutes before.

'I'll bring you something cool to drink,' Ariana offered. 'Would you like orange juice or *ouzo* and one of Aunt Evadne's honey cakes?'

'*Ouzo* and honey cakes would be fine,' he decided. 'Then I won't have to stop somewhere for lunch.'

Rhea followed her cousin to the kitchen where

Evadne was preparing a colourful Greek salad for their own midday meal.

'What did Nicolas want?' she asked bluntly, although it was obvious that she must have heard a good deal of their conversation through the open window. 'He has been here already one hour, and I have not known him to stay so long when he was calling on business.'

'He has offered to take us to Delphi on his way to Agrinion tomorrow.' Ariana filled a jug of water at the sink, setting it down on a tray beside a bottle of the local wine before she collected four tall glasses from one of the cupboards above her head. 'Can we have some honey cakes, Aunt Evadne, and—will you join us?' she asked as an afterthought. 'It is almost eleven o'clock.'

'Delphi?' Evadne was repeating. 'But that must be out of his way.'

'Not very far,' Ariana decided. 'It only means going into the mountains instead of taking the coast road, and Nicolas has a powerful car.'

'A very fast one,' her aunt returned drily, her thin lips firming into a disapproving line. 'When was this arranged?'

'Only a moment ago,' Ariana told her. 'He offered to take us because the Buggy has to have an overhaul to make it fit for the road. Grandpapa agrees,' she added emphatically, as if that should end all argument, as, indeed, it seemed to do.

'I have no time to stop for *ouzo* and honey cakes,' Evadne informed them, although her suspicious eyes followed their every movement on their way back to the terrace with the refreshments.

'Are you going to try our local wine?' John Karousis asked. 'It may take you some time to acquire a taste for it and it will be best for you diluted with water. Ariana drinks only orange juice, which is more fitting for her age.'

'Grandpapa!' Ariana admonished. 'You *do* think I am still a child.'

'So—what else must I consider you, fresh out of school?' the old man teased, pouring a small portion of *ouzo* from the bottle into two of the glasses. 'Nicolas, we

will take ours neat, like men!' He poured another
measure for Rhea, pushing the water jug across the
table towards her. 'If you must,' he said, 'you can dilute
it with that.'

As she poured the sparkling spring water into the
wine it changed colour dramatically, swirling into a
white, cloudy liquid which gradually cleared as more
water was added.

'Now you have spoiled it!' the old man laughed, the
wrinkles deepening round his eyes. 'It will have no
flavour at all.'

Ariana poured her own orange juice, passing round
the honey cakes as Rhea sipped the wine.

'Well?' her grandfather demanded. 'What do you
think?'

Rhea hesitated, suddenly aware that they were being
watched by Evadne from the kitchen window.

'I'm not sure,' she had to admit. 'It's like drinking
distilled aniseed, but I suppose I'll come to like it in
time.'

'It is very good for you,' her grandfather declared
roguishly. 'You must notice how fit we all are after
drinking it for most of our lives!'

'If it isn't exactly nectar it's the next best thing, he
means!' Nicolas laughed. 'Don't drink it, Rhea, if you
don't like it. I wouldn't exactly recommend it as the
nectar of the gods!'

'I'll have to try again,' Rhea decided, putting down
her glass. 'I would hate to fall at the very first hurdle.'

He rose to his feet.

'Somehow, I don't think you will.' He turned to take
his leave of the family as Phaedra Karousis came across
the terrace towards them, smiling broadly. '*Kaliméra*,
Kyria Karousis!' he greeted her, bending over her
gnarled, extended hand. 'Alas! I am ready to leave, but
I have a message for you from my mother. Will you
come to Florina one day soon and take coffee with her?'

'She is not often there,' Phaedra said, shaking her
head, although she seemed pleased by the invitation.
'We must arrange it,' she added slowly.

'Until tomorrow!' Nicholas turned on his heel to

leave. 'I will pick you up at eight,' he said to the two girls.

Rhea watched her grandfather escort him to the end of the terrace where the convertible stood waiting for him at the foot of the steps. They were both strong, handsome men, one in the prime of his youth, the other bent a little with age, but both with the same sense of humour and dedication to their heritage. She felt that Nicolas Metaxas would work as earnestly and as hard for Florina as her grandfather had done for Volponé through many years of war and depression, husbanding it for future generations yet unborn, meeting disappointment when it came with a stiffened lip and joy in its turn with a smile. Already she loved her grandfather, although she had known him for less than twenty-four hours.

She turned to the woman who had been his wife for almost fifty years.

'Grandmama,' she offered, 'can I pour you some wine?'

'I will take the fruit juice,' Phaedra Karousis said carefully. '*Ouzo* no longer agrees with my stomach.'

Ariana filled a glass for her, carrying the jug back to the kitchen where Evadne was still at work.

'A honey cake?' Rhea offered her grandmother the half-empty plate. 'They are delicious!'

Phaedra shook her head.

'But you——' she said, struggling with the language she hardly knew.

'I have eaten three already!' Rhea sat contentedly at her feet, breathing in the heavy scent of honeysuckle while she listened to the hum of bees. 'It is lovely here,' she said, at last. 'Very much as I expected.' She looked up into the wrinkled face, meeting the dark eyes squarely. 'Can you tell me about my mother?' she asked.

Phaedra hesitated, thinking deeply, and then, suddenly, she rose to her feet and began to walk away.

'*Me sinchorite!*' she said, turning as she reached the kitchen door. 'You wait here.'

Rhea sat down on the marble terrace wall where the

vine made a dappled pattern of sun and shade on the
flags at her feet, thinking how easy it was to wait in
such idyllic surroundings where time itself seemed to
rest. She could hear Ariana and Evadne talking in the
kitchen, but their voices sounded very far away and she
hoped that her cousin would not return immediately to
interrupt the tête-à-tête she wished to have with her
grandmother.

The old lady returned with a leather wallet in her
hand, sitting down on the bench beside her, but she
didn't open it immediately. Instead, she sat gazing
across the terrace to the garden where the oleanders
made a hedge of scarlet blossom between them and the
olive grove, thinking her own thoughts as she retraced
her footsteps into the past. When she finally opened the
wallet she drew out a photograph, faded now with the
passing years.

'Your mother,' she said briefly. 'Maria Karousis.'

Rhea had seen a photograph of her mother before,
one her father had taken in England before she was
born and another with her baby on her knee that first
year in the garden in London, but this one was of a
younger and more lighthearted Maria, a girl with long
dark hair framing her face and dancing eyes which
reflected Grandpapa Karousis's teasing smile. The girl
her father had met and fallen in love with at first sight!
But Maria was not alone. She was with someone else, a
big, heavily-bearded man who reminded her instantly
of Nicolas Metaxas.

It could be Nicolas's father, she realised, her breath
catching in her throat, the discarded lover of all those
long years ago who had married someone else on the
rebound.

Phaedra Karousis did not explain who he was.

'Did you like my father?' Rhea asked cautiously.

They sat for a long time in the dappled shade before
her grandmother answered her.

'We accepted him,' the old lady said, at last.

It was the reason for the reserve in her, Rhea
thought, and part of the reason for Evadne's open
hostility, but they had welcomed her on her first adult

visit to Greece because she was 'family' and that was encouraging. Given time, perhaps she could win them over completely and ensure their unquestioning love.

Given time, she repeated inwardly, but had she really enough time to convince them of her worth? She wanted so desperately to belong, to be part of a happy family again, but perhaps she was asking too much. She sat with her grandmother in silence, listening to the languorous sounds of the farmyard until the old lady murmured her excuses and moved away to help in the kitchen.

They ate their midday meal on the terrace sheltered from the strengthening sun by the thickness of the vines, and when it was over John Karousis fell asleep, his chin cushioned on his ample white beard, his eyes closed in blissful slumber while Evadne and Ariana cleared away the remnants of the meal and Rhea went with her grandmother to feed the goats. It was difficult to converse for any length of time, but the old lady grew more and more relaxed as they walked under the trees, standing from time to time to admire the view. It seemed that Phaedra Karousis would never tire of looking out over the narrow valley to the distant mountains which encircled her home.

Their tasks in the house completed, Ariana came in search of her cousin.

'Would you like to go swimming, Rhea?' she asked. 'You heard Nicolas say that we could use the pool at Florina whenever we liked,' she rushed on, 'and it will be cool there. There is no wind,' she added as an extra inducement, 'and we will be alone.'

'Are you sure we won't be disturbing anyone?' Rhea asked, thinking about Nicolas's mother.

'The pool is a short distance from the house,' Ariana assured her, 'and Kyria Metaxas is not likely to be there. If she is, she will be busy in the house and will not see us. Do let us go, Rhea,' she added earnestly. 'It's a day for swimming in the sun, you must agree!'

They ran upstairs to collect their swimsuits, putting them on under towelling wraps with canvas *espadrilles* on their feet in order to walk through the olive grove on the first stage of their journey.

'I've told Aunt Evadne where we're going and she will explain to Grandpapa when he wakes up,' Ariana said. 'He likes to know where everyone is while he smokes his pipe in the shade!'

The Persian cat followed them to the edge of the olive grove, pretending indifference and keeping in the shade.

'Go back, Artemis!' Ariana commanded. 'We are going to swim.'

The yellow, baleful eyes followed them as they walked on, plunging into the thicker shade of the scented grove where butterflies fluttered expectantly and the hum of bees filled the air with lethargic sound.

Ariana walked quickly, eager to reach Florina and the swimming-pool, but Rhea would have lingered in the shaded grove for a very long time, wondering if her mother had come this way often when she had been going to Florina to visit her future in-laws. It must have seemed an ideal situation between the two families whose land adjoined each other's, and whose interests must have been the same. And then her father had come along and changed everything!

They climbed the narrow path on to the plateau, meeting a little wind that came from the north.

'When the *meltémi* blows it can be cold up here,' Ariana said, 'but the trees give much shelter. Soon we will be going down into the woods and then up again to Florina. You will see it long before we come to it, standing on the ridge.'

It was another half-hour before they caught a first glimpse of the house Rhea had only seen from a distance earlier in the day. It stood above a row of terraces, its white stucco glaring in the light of the sun, its sheltering trees standing back to afford it an uninterrupted view right down the valley to the encircling mountains in the north, an old house reminiscent of the Roman villas which had been scattered across an empire long ago, a house with charm and personality looking down towards Volponé with mildly friendly eyes.

The road they had taken across the escarpment was narrow and weed-covered and their feet threw up the pungent scent of crushed thyme as they walked, but the forest trees provided all the shelter they needed from the fierce afternoon sun. Long before they had reached the house itself Ariana turned aside.

'We go down here,' she said. 'The pool is just below the terraces.'

A deep declivity in the land had made it easy to construct a sizeable pool at one side of the house and over the years a high hedge of laurel had grown up to screen it from the prevailing wind. Constructed of ancient stone and faced with marble, it looked ideally part of the surroundings, while the terraces which stepped down from the house itself were ablaze with roses of every kind and hue. Blue, clear water sparkled in the sun, inviting them in.

'It's filled by a mountain spring,' Ariana told her, 'so it is always fresh and clear.'

It had been hot walking all the way from Volponé, and for a short time they rested in the shade of a small changing-room built in the form of a Roman temple at the far end of the pool. One concession to artificiality, its slender marble columns and domed roof did not look out of place in its setting of laurel and it served its purpose very well. Otherwise, the garden was a series of terraces linked by rows of steps in the traditional Greek manner, shrubs and flowers and trees lending their seasonal colour to the scene as if they had grown there since the beginning of time.

'Nicolas's mother planned the garden,' Ariana explained. 'She is a lover of colour and her favourite flower is the rose. It is all very beautiful, would you say?'

Rhea was looking towards the house.

'Are you sure there's no one there?' she asked. 'I thought I saw someone a moment ago.'

'They have a man who looks after the garden— Stavros,' Ariana explained, 'and several people helping in the house. It could have been Stavros or Melina you saw. They are always around.'

Rhea accepted the fact that it could have been Melina, taking off her towelling beach-coat to dive into the pool after her cousin.

'Wow!' The water had taken her breath away. In spite of the sun blazing down on the sheltered pool for most of the morning, it was still cold, but gloriously refreshing. 'I didn't expect it to be so—invigorating.'

'It's always like this,' her cousin told her, swimming alongside. 'In a moment or two you'll be glowing all over. It's just the first plunge that surprises you and, remember, we were very warm by the time we got here.'

They swam for half an hour, diving from the side of the pool or from the spring board at its far end, and finally lying on their backs to float luxuriously with the sun on their faces and a pleasant, warm glow spreading over their bodies as they relaxed.

'Are you enjoying yourselves?'

The voice came from the terraced steps above them, a woman's voice, clear and distinct, speaking in English. Rhea turned over to find herself looking up at a tall, slim woman in a brightly-printed kaftan with her dark hair swathed in a red chiffon scarf and her feet thrust into comfortable blue *espadrilles*. In her youth she must have been very lovely with those penetrating dark eyes and the classical beauty of a face which, even now, was only lightly marked with the lines of stress. The firm mouth was half parted in a smile to show two rows of excellent white teeth, although the eyes were decidedly watchful. Rhea knew who she was before her cousin had time to introduce them.

'Kyria Metaxas, this is my cousin from England,' she said, hoisting herself to the edge of the pool to squint up at their hostess in the sun. 'Rhea,' she added, 'I'd like you to meet Nicolas's mother.'

Surprise had been Rhea's first reaction because she had already conjured up a picture of a comfortable, middle-aged woman, a younger edition of Phaedra Karousis, with a homely look about her and possibly dressed entirely in black as befitted her widowed state. This was something entirely different, she decided, getting out of the pool to shake hands.

'I'm rather wet,' she apologised, shaking back her dripping hair as she attempted to dry at least her hand on the towelling beach coat. 'Excuse me!'

Alexandra Metaxas was studying her closely.

'Nicolas told me you might come,' she said in her highly accented English, 'and I supposed this afternoon would be warm enough for you.' The hand she extended was long and beautifully manicured, her smile suitably welcoming as they stood on the edge of the pool. It was only the darkly penetrating gaze which seemed to question Rhea's presence there. Ariana she seemed to take for granted. 'What do you think of Greece, Miss Langford?' she asked. 'Does it come up to your expectations?'

'I think it's beautiful, even if I haven't seen very much of it so far.' Rhea slipped into her towelling coat, feeling more respectable that way. 'I had no idea about your mountains.'

'Your mother's mountains, too,' Alexandra Metaxas reminded her. 'You have come to discover your Greek heritage, I suppose. I think you will love our country after you have been here for a while. After all, your poet, Byron, considered it to be his spiritual home, didn't he?' she added lightly.

'He died fighting for Greece,' Rhea reflected. 'It was all rather sad, I thought, because he was so young.'

Alexandra sat down on the marble steps above the pool, clasping her long fingers about her knees.

'Nicolas tells me he is taking you to Delphi tomorrow,' she said after a moment's thought. 'It is something you must not miss, but don't let the village itself put you off. It is the usual conglomeration of tourist trap and jazz music, I'm afraid; very greatly commercialised and not in any way beautiful except for its incomparable situation. The mountains overwhelm it, thank goodness, and the Parnassos country is worthy of a look, to say nothing of the Tholos, which may disturb you. But there,' she added with her attractive smile which was so reminiscent of her son's, 'don't let me inflict my jaded opinion on the first flush of your enthusiasm! Go and see for yourself.'

It was as if she had given them her blessing, Rhea thought, an older woman concerned about the younger generation's appreciation of the land she had always loved.

'Come up to the house when you are ready,' she invited, getting nimbly to her feet. 'As you know, Ariana, I drink tea at four o'clock.'

It was an English custom which she must have adopted in spite of the traditional way of Greek life she had probably led for a very long time, one picked up in Athens, no doubt, where it had become popular after the Second World War.

'It's very good of you, Kyria Metaxas,' Rhea acknowledged respectfully.

'Not at all.' Alexandra gave her another long, searching look. 'After all, you are Nicolas's guests.'

Was she anxious to see who her son had invited to their home after such a short acquaintance, or was it something that went deeper than that? She was the woman who had come afterwards, the woman Nicolas's father had married on the rebound, perhaps, after Maria had given him up. Nothing in her present manner, however, suggested that she considered herself aggrieved by the knowledge that she had not been first in her husband's affections in the beginning. She had a calmly assured air, and that smile could never have concealed uncertainty.

Ariana said, 'You'll love the house, Rhea. She hasn't changed it. Only the garden. Nicolas's father was born and brought up here and Nicolas also. A family home is very precious in Greece, something always to come back to. Kyria Metaxas isn't always here, of course. She is a very busy person and must have somewhere in Athens in order to entertain. It is a long way to travel daily between here and Athens, you understand, but she is at home most weekends.'

'She doesn't go to the island?' Rhea asked, surprised.

'Not very often. She leaves Nicolas to concentrate on the dig because she thinks it's good for him to have a hobby and to relax away from business.'

'What does she do in Athens?' Rhea asked.

'Oh, I thought I'd told you!' Ariana said on their way up the steps. 'She has a shop. Her father was a successful silversmith and jeweller and she has carried on the business. She is also an artist and makes beautiful things. Some of them are her own designs and some are copies of old artefacts which have been found in Greece.'

'Like my necklet,' Rhea suggested. 'I wonder if her firm made the copy all these years ago? But then, I don't suppose they did. It would be too much of a coincidence, since there must be more than one silversmith's in Athens.'

'There are many,' Ariana agreed. 'Many jewellers, I mean, but they are not all craftsmen. When we go to Athens we must visit Kyria Metaxas's shop. It is in one of the finest streets. How do you say? She is in business in a very grand way.'

They had reached the top of the steps and were facing the lovely old house, which looked much larger than it had done from the forest road. Long windows dominated the paved terrace on to which they opened, and on the upper storey the stone balcony must have afforded magnificent views right down the entire valley to the mountains beyond. Alexandra Metaxas was waiting for them at an open window and she stepped out on to the terrace as they approached.

'We will take tea here,' she suggested, indicating the wrought iron table and chairs which were set out on the mosaic slabs in the shade afforded by a magnificent magnolia in a giant tub. 'This is our best view and I never tire of looking at the mountains.'

Rhea sat down on one of the deep cane loungers with an appreciative sigh.

'No wonder you love your home, Kyria Metaxas,' she said. 'You even have a cooling breeze up here.'

'Sometimes we need it—in high summer, for instance—although we could do without the *meltémi* when it blows,' Alexandra said. 'That is something quite different, when we sometimes fear for our roof! You will not be troubled with it while you are here, of course. Spring is the right time to come to Greece, when it is neither too hot nor too inclement because of rain. How long will you stay, do you think?'

'I thought—about a month,' Rhea told her uncertainly.

'Surely more than that?' Alexandra protested. 'You have so much to see. When Ariana regains her car you must come to Athens and we will show you round.'

'I have been trying to persuade her to help on the dig,' Ariana said, 'but she will not agree without much thought.'

Alexandra looked sharply in Rhea's direction.

'Why is that?' she asked. 'Surely you must be interested when your father was so keen?'

'I'd love to go——' Rhea hesitated. 'It's just that there are so many things to do first. I—you see, I've never been on a dig before, and I might be in the way.'

'Nonsense!' declared Alexandra. 'According to Nicolas, everyone is capable of doing *something*. I'd be of more help to him, I suppose, if I didn't want to rush off and copy those marvellous trinkets they find from time to time. You know he has opened up the original excavations? My husband lost interest in them after we married, I'm afraid, but Nicolas believes there is still much to find.'

A maid came from the house with a large tray which her mistress helped her to set on the table.

'Thank you, Semele,' she said. 'What have you managed to find for us to eat?'

'Honey cakes and bread!' the young girl beamed, proud that she could answer the question in English. 'Do you wish more?'

'This will do, thank you,' Alexandra said, setting out the fine bone china. 'I think there is plenty here for us all.' She poured the tea from a lovely old Georgian teapot. 'Will you take lemon or milk?'

'Lemon, please,' Rhea said.

While she passed their cups Alexandra studied Rhea unashamedly.

'I wondered if you would be like Daphne,' she said as she offered the sugar-bowl across the table, 'but you are not in the least like her. Have you met yet?'

'No.' Rhea could not make up her mind whether Kyria Metaxas liked her cousin or not. 'We passed each other briefly at the airport when I came in.'

'Nicolas was seeing her off to somewhere or other,' Ariana explained.

'Rome, I expect.' Alexandra frowned. 'She is never in Athens for more than five minutes these days, but that's as it should be, I suppose. She has a great ambition to succeed at her profession, if being a model for fashionable clothes can be called that. Ah, well, each to his own! We shall see how it all turns out in the end, but I can't help wishing that she had stayed in her own country. There is plenty of scope for that sort of thing in Athens just like anywhere else, but Rome seems to be somewhat of a Mecca nowadays and the money is better.'

Her criticism of Daphne ended there. They spoke of other things: of the delights of sailing among the Islands during the summer months and bathing in the sea from the numerous sandy beaches strung out along the coast; of sight-seeing among the mountains and shopping in Athens while it was still cool enough to walk.

When the shadows began to lengthen across the terrace they rose to go.

'We have stayed longer than we should have done,' Ariana apologised, 'and tomorrow we must rise early to be ready when Nicolas comes to collect us.'

'You will be safer with him than in that car of yours!' Alexandra teased, walking with them to the terrace edge. 'Have a pleasant day!'

Before they reached the olive grove the sun had drawn down to the west staining the whole sky in a brilliant red glow and touching the mountain tops with fire. The brilliant light lay across the valley like an embrazened shield, making trees and houses and distant escarpments stand out against it like dark etchings on a copper plate. Rhea held her breath.

'I had no idea it would be like this,' she said. 'It's almost unbelievable. I could stay here for hours!'

'Better not,' laughed Ariana. 'We would have to answer to Aunt Evadne if we did.'

'She must miss Daphne living in the house,' Rhea reflected. 'But she must be proud of her daughter being so much in demand.'

'It's difficult to know what Aunt Evadne thinks,' Ariana returned. 'She does not wear her heart on her jacket.'

' "On her sleeve",' Rhea corrected, smilingly. 'Yes, I think you are right. It may be because she has never had anyone to confide in, but Kyria Metaxas also thought that Daphne should return to Greece.'

'She is equally patriotic,' Ariana said, 'and she may see Daphne as a future daughter-in-law.'

Remembering the searching look in Alexandra Metaxas's eyes when they had first met, Rhea could not dismiss the possibility even although Alexandra had appeared to criticise her cousin for staying away.

'Daphne comes and goes,' Ariana reflected. 'It's a nomadic life being an international model, I understand.' They had reached the end of the hill road and come to the terrace above the olive grove. 'This has always been the barrier between Volpone and Florina. No! Once again I have used the wrong word,' she amended. 'Should I not have said "boundary"?'

Rhea looked down at the silent grove of olives. Barrier or boundary, it seemed to be something which both families had laid claim to in the past, a narrow tract of land lying in deep shade now that the sunshine had gone. It was part of the valley floor, fertile land that could have grown crops or more productive trees and perhaps it was only natural for Nicolas Metaxas to think of it in terms of timber.

They reached Volponé as the light faded, casting a pale pink colour over the white stone. It was still warm enough to have lingered in the garden, but Ariana thought she should help with the evening meal. When Rhea made her way up the shallow stairs to the floor above Evadne was standing at her bedroom door.

'I have brought you fresh towels,' she announced. 'You will find them on your bed.' She stood her ground as Rhea entered the room. 'How long do you intend to stay here?' she asked.

Utterly surprised and shaken by the question, Rhea paused beside the bed.

'I've only just arrived,' she pointed out defensively. 'Why do you ask?'

'I like to know where I stand.'

'Because of the extra work?' Rhea asked. 'But I have offered to help, Aunt Evadne. I will do my share because I don't really consider myself a guest in the less intimate sense of the word.'

'We do not need your help,' her aunt said stiffly. 'My father is very old and very——' She hesitated. 'I do not know your word for it, but he is foolish sometimes when he thinks about the past.'

'Perhaps "sentimental" is the word you want,' Rhea suggested, 'but isn't that quite natural? After all, my mother was his daughter.'

A swift flush ran up under her aunt's sallow skin.

'She left Greece to make her home elsewhere. She married an Englishman.'

'My father,' Rhea said. 'If it would be any comfort to you, Aunt Evadne, they were very happy together.'

'Comfort!' Her aunt's eyes narrowed. 'I do not need "comfort" of that sort. My sister deserted her family when she went to England to make a new life there. That is all we know.'

'She must have written to you from time to time.'

Evadne's gaze remained fixed on a point beyond her head.

'Once—perhaps twice,' she allowed. 'We did not answer her letters.'

'How cruel!' Rhea's reaction was involuntary. 'She must have needed you more than ever when she found herself in a strange country.'

'She had your father,' Evadne reminded her without pity.

'They were very much in love.' Rhea found herself repeating the fact as her mother's ultimate defence. 'I believe they knew that as soon as they met.'

'Maria was already to marry someone else!'

'Yes. She was engaged to Nicolas's father, but it doesn't seem to make much difference now. I have just met Kyria Metaxas at Florina, where we went to swim, and she was charming.'

Evadne laughed.

'Alexandra Metaxas is always charming, but she is like a cat who watches with half-closed eyes. You would do well to beware of her. She has many plans for Florina, and for her son.'

A hot colour ran into Rhea's cheeks.

'Mothers generally do,' she returned swiftly. 'They want only the best for their children, I'm sure.'

'She hopes one day he will own our land,' Evadne said carefully, 'and he will do that by marrying either Ariana or Daphne, whom you have yet to meet. She has gone to Rome, but she is still joint heiress with Ariana because all my father's sons were killed defending their country in many senseless wars. Girls can inherit in Greece, you understand, so my father has no need of a male heir.'

It wasn't difficult to see her bitterness at never having had a son to inherit Volponé, and for a moment Rhea felt genuinely sorry for her, and then she was remembering the girl she had first glimpsed with Nicolas Metaxas at Athens airport and she was aware of a vague regret. Of course, her cousin Daphne was right for Nicolas—right in so many ways. She was the personification of everything Greek, a goddess in the mould of Athena and Eurydice, with a suggestion of Circe thrown in for tantalising measure!

It was foolish to think of her absent cousin in this way, she supposed, foolish and self-destructive if she was ever to look on Nicolas as her friend.

Evadne turned away along the darkened corridor, going silently, like a watchful cat.

CHAPTER THREE

ARIANA tapped at Rhea's door early the following morning.

'Wake up! All the cocks are crowing and the sun is over the mountain rim,' she announced. 'It is going to be another lovely day.'

Rubbing the sleep out of her eyes, Rhea crossed to the shutters to let in the light and was suddenly bathed in a golden glow.

'Don't tell me Nicolas is here already!' she smiled.

'Oh, no! It's still early, but we must tidy our rooms before we go. I heard Aunt Evadne complaining about the extra work to Grandmama while I was helping in the kitchen last night. She will use any weapon she finds to discredit us, you understand, because she is angry about Daphne.'

'Daphne?'

'About her not being here—about her preferring to have a flat in Athens and working so much in Rome.'

'Surely she's old enough to choose for herself.' Rhea slipped into the cotton dress she had decided to wear for their trip to Delphi. 'She must be over twenty-one.'

'She is twenty-three. One year older than you are yourself and three years younger than Nicolas.'

Nicolas Metaxas's name was cropping up everywhere, Rhea thought.

'Should I take a woollen coat?' she asked.

'Perhaps it would be as well. We might even return in the dark,' Ariana speculated romantically. 'That would be if Nicolas took us for a meal afterwards. You should really have a meal in a taverna,' she added. 'It's lots of fun.'

When they went downstairs together Nicolas had arrived. He was standing at the far end of the terrace talking earnestly to John Karousis, and Rhea's heart seemed to miss a beat as she wondered what had gone wrong.

'Do you think he's come to say we can't go?' she whispered to Ariana.

'No. They always talk like that when they meet. It is mostly about politics or the state of the drachma. Nothing important, you understand.'

Nicolas turned at the sound of their voices.

'*Kaliméra!*' he greeted them. 'I hear you were at Florina yesterday and enjoyed your swim.' He was looking directly at Rhea, appraising her with those magnetic eyes. 'My mother offered you tea, I understand. It is a weakness of hers.'

'Which we greatly appreciated, although we were both straight out of the pool and very wet,' Rhea smiled, looking into his blue, appraising eyes. 'I'm looking forward to our trip to Delphi,' she added. 'Thank you very much for suggesting it.'

'You would have gone sooner or later,' he assured her, 'because it really is a must for visitors to Greece. Have you packed a picnic lunch?'

'Ariana has something in a basket.'

'Good! It's much better than having a meal in a café on a day like this—even a café in Delphi!'

He turned to say goodbye to her grandfather, and Rhea was suddenly aware of Evadne watching again from the kitchen window. Her aunt did not come to say goodbye or wish them a pleasant day. Instead she busied herself noisily with her domestic tasks, making it quite plain that someone had to work. Ariana and Rhea kissed John Karousis on both cheeks.

'What a lot we'll have to tell you when we return!' Rhea smiled. 'I wish you were coming with us.'

'I have no need to consult an oracle about my future,' he told her, smiling. 'Most of my wishes are in the past, but I will wait to hear all about your visit and what happened when you got there. Meanwhile, I will sit at home and smoke my pipe, *not* wishing for the moon!'

When the car was started Ariana looked up at one of the first-floor windows.

'There's Grandmama,' she said, 'waving to us.'

Nicolas drove quite fast, and soon they were on the road to Thebes with a great escarpment towering above them and mountains far away. Wild flowers grew everywhere on the green hillsides, and the fields nearer at hand were carpeted with glowing red tulips for most of the way.

'We ski near here in the winter,' Ariana told her. 'On the other side of Parnassos.'

Snow glinted near the mountaintops ahead of them, white against the incredibly blue sky, and Rhea fell silent, awed by the grandeur of mountains, gorges and rivers which was suddenly revealed to them. Then, turning sharply away from the magical vista of sea and plain and fast-flowing rivers, Nicolas steered the grey convertible towards the highest mountain of all. They were on the slopes of Parnassos and almost at their destination, winding by a spectacular series of hairpin bends through the long, narrow and lovely valley to Delphi by the Sacred Way of the ancients. Even Ariana was silenced by the splendour all round them, although she must have seen it many times before.

The air became more rarefied as they climbed upwards and the scenery more awesome. They passed through a dizzily-perched village where woollen handicrafts were displayed at every door, turning sharply at the last of the houses to climb again up Mount Parnassos. Nicolas drew into the side of the road to let them enjoy the view.

'I—it's beyond believing!' Rhea gasped. 'I had no idea it would be like this.'

Nicolas smiled.

'I've made up my mind to go all the way with you,' he announced. 'Your disbelief is infectious!'

'Incredulity,' she corrected him. 'Nicolas, thank you for bringing me.'

He drove on, down a gradual descent through a deep gorge which opened out into a sea of olive trees dazzled by the sun where a great cliff seemed to bar their way until they had rounded it successfully and Delphi came into view.

'We'll leave the car in the village,' Nicolas decided, 'and walk from there.'

Little terraced houses clung to the rock, gazing down into the gorge where the silver stream of the Pleistos wound between a narrow strip of olive trees flanked by a precipitous cliff, while beyond it the whole Sacred Plain lay, green and fertile, in the golden sunlight. Above the ruined sanctuary the cliffs of the Phaedriads rose sternly, cleft by a narrow chasm which seemed to hold all the shadows of the world, imprisoning them for ever. The absolute grandeur of the place, the mountains and the deep, silent gorges and the still, white ruins of the Temple itself kept speech at bay, and Rhea, who had longed to come here, had never expected anything like this.

They left the car at one of the hotels in the modern village where a single main street marched between restaurants and cafés and souvenir shops offering their tawdry wares in abundance beside brightly-coloured woollen rugs from Arachova and other local crafts.

When they began to climb towards the sanctuary itself Ariana lagged a little way behind. The monuments and temples of the Marmaria were built on steep terraces, but she could not possibly be tired, Rhea decided, since they had just started to walk and it couldn't be any great distance. They waited for her to catch up.

'I had a stone in my shoe,' she explained. 'It's rubbed my heel.'

They explored the sanctuary with its ruined temples, and the foundations of old monuments extending across the slope and Nicolas explained the excavations which had been carried out by the French arch-aeologists.

'It must have been a fulfilling task,' he mused, 'but— all this makes me wonder why I'm bothering to dig on the island. We haven't found very much so far, nothing of great importance, but I suppose there can be a sense of achievement in smaller finds. Your father felt that way, I believe, and so did mine.'

'It's all coming very near,' Rhea confessed as they passed the remains of a Roman portico. 'I think I'm beginning to understand how he felt. Just beginning,' she mused, 'because it was the preoccupation of a lifetime. He went to Egypt, you know, during the last few years of his life, although he never returned to Greece.'

They walked along the narrow Sacred Way to the shrine of Apollo, climbing a zigzag path flanked on either side by the bases of statues long since removed or destroyed, towards a small Doric temple obviously reconstructed from the original marble blocks lying on the spot. It stood out against the confusion of foundations and trenches and scattered stone, drawing the eye away from the ruined seat of the Oracle in the very centre of the shrine.

It was difficult to stand there and not feel the distant past washing over you, Rhea thought, feeling her father's nearness as never before, and falling silent again as they turned away from the ancient seat of prophecy to explore the Stadium and the theatre which dominated Apollo's temple and the whole sanctuary.

They sat on a sun-warmed stone on the last tier of the terracing looking out over the convulsed landscape which enclosed it, and Ariana flopped down beside them, evidently having walked far enough.

'It's after twelve o'clock,' she pointed out. 'Time we had something to eat.'

They shared the contents of her basket in the shade of an olive tree on one of the terraces of the Marmaria, eating the crisp brown bread Evadne had baked the day before generously spread with *taramasaláta*, and small canapés crowned with red caviar which Ariana called *brik*.

'It's far too hot to go on walking,' she announced, taking off her shoe. 'Already I have a blister on my heel.'

Nicolas looked at Rhea, sensing her disappointment.

'How do you feel?' he asked.

'Perhaps we can come back some other time,' she suggested. 'It *is* very hot.'

'You could spend an hour at the museum,' Ariana suggested. 'Then, when it's cooler, we could walk up here again.'

They quenched their considerable thirst at the Kastalian spring where it gushed out of a narrow chasm between the twin Phaedriades, shunning the cafés under the plane trees which were now crowded with people on tour.

'It's going to be a long, hot climb back to the museum,' Nicolas pointed out. 'Is there anything else you would like to see?'

Rhea looked down through the olive trees to the path leading back to the terraces of the Marmaria.

'Could we go to the Tholos?' she asked. 'It wouldn't take very long.'

'Tell you what,' Ariana suggested. 'Nicolas can take you while I hobble back to the village and sit in the car. I've had the Marmaria for one day, but I think you should go and see some more ruins before we leave!'

'Will you come?' Nicolas was looking at Rhea intently. 'It isn't very far.'

Rhea went without thought, walking with him in the sunshine into a new experience.

Surrounded by mountains and shaded by ancient trees, the Tholos stood in full and brilliant sunshine, a round Doric temple whose circular base rose among ruined steps and truncated columns into the pure, thin air. The silence around it could almost be felt as they walked between the scattered stones, their eyes fixed on the three slender columns which had been lovingly restored and now stood out in spectacular beauty against the bare mountainside. Nicolas had taken Rhea by the hand to help her up the last incline and he kept her fingers imprisoned in his as they stood there breathing in the pure mountain air and listening to the silences. Because it was now the lunch hour and the sun was very hot they were alone on the terrace. Time was theirs to do with as they willed.

The atmosphere around them was more bucolic and far more gentle than the approach to the sanctuary, and a little breeze strayed through the tracery of trees to cool their cheeks. Rhea put her free hand to her forehead to brush aside the strand of hair which had blown across her eyes. Why was she alone with Nicolas on Parnassos, high above the world? Because Ariana had a stone in her shoe, or because the wayward gods had decreed it? Her head felt light and her heart began to beat madly against her breast. Was she falling in love again?

She pushed the thought away from her, but it was still there when they finally climbed higher to see the little temple from a different viewpoint, looking beyond it to a sky flecked with a single cloud.

They did not speak, standing there, hand in hand, letting the minutes slip away until time itself had gone. The stillness, the sense of awe in the hushed atmosphere wrapped them round, drawing them close and at last he drew her fully into his arms.

'Rhea, you've made it all new for me,' he said quietly. 'It's been a wonderful moment for us both.'

She stood in the circle of his imprisoning arms as he kissed her and she gave him back kiss for kiss, passionately and unreservedly, as she had never done in all her life before, without thought, her senses swimming in a sea of unreality as his dark head blotted out the full brilliance of the sun. They were here, alone.

They became aware of the group of sightseers coming up the hill towards them.

'The magic's gone,' he said, freeing her reluctantly. 'We are no longer alone on Parnassos, Rhea. We must go down.'

'Ariana will be waiting for us,' Rhea said.

The world will be waiting for us, she meant. This could only be a folly, a scene out of Paradise where they had lingered for a moment in the sun. What were they both doing there—Nicolas, the hard-headed business-man and she who had been so determined not to fall in love a second time? Not to be hurt by love.

She was trembling when he took her hand again to lead her down from that high place where all these ancient gods had seemed to smile on them.

Ariana was waiting for them at the Xenia hotel situated on a cliff dominating the gorge.

'I've done some shopping,' she announced with a

satisfied smile. 'I had to walk through the village, you understand.'

'You needn't excuse yourself,' Nicolas assured her. 'Can I leave you here for an hour while I got on to Agrinion?' he asked. 'I have to justify all this driving among the mountains by picking up some business on the way!'

It was his original destination, Rhea remembered, before he had gone out of his way to bring them to Delphi.

'We'll laze around and have something to drink while we wait,' Ariana said, 'and maybe we can walk back along the village to look at the shops.'

He ordered cooling drinks for them, driving off as they stood looking down across the gorge to the plain below.

'Did you enjoy your walk to the Tholos?' Ariana asked, looking over the rim of her glass. 'Did it come up to your expectations?'

Rhea turned her back, presumably intent on the view.

'I—didn't have any expectations,' she said. 'I had no idea what the Tholos looked like.'

'I wasn't talking about the Tholos,' Ariana said. 'I wondered how you got on with Nicolas.'

Rhea turned to look at her.

'You planned it!' she accused. 'You hadn't a stone in your shoe at all.'

'Oh, I had,' Ariana contradicted her. 'It just didn't skin my heel, that was all!'

'You're impossible!'

Ariana gave her a little smile.

'Why impossible?' she asked. 'I do not wish to see Nicolas married to our cousin Daphne, and he was looking at you in such an interested way.'

A deep flush of embarrassment stained Rhea's cheeks.

'You are far too romantic,' she accused the smiling Ariana. 'You didn't know the first thing about Nicolas—nor me.'

'I can guess.' Ariana sipped her orange juice. 'And I know that Nicolas is kind and very generous, and he could quite easily fall in love with you if Daphne kept away.'

'That's quite ridiculous!' The colour had deepened in Rhea's cheeks. 'People don't fall in love to order, you know.'

Ariana examined her half-empty glass.

'That's true,' she allowed. 'I know the circumstances have to be right, but Delphi *is* romantic, don't you think?'

'Very,' Rhea agreed drily. 'Do you think your injured foot might make it as far as the end of the village street?' she added. 'It isn't far to walk.'

Ariana drained the last of the orange juice.

'You won't like it,' she predicted, 'after the Tholos!'

They spent an hour at the shops, ending up in a café where the proprietor regaled his customers with jazz music to accompany the coffee and honey cakes which were his speciality.

'We'd better make our way back to the hotel,' Ariana yelled in her ear. 'It's getting late.'

Nicolas drew up behind them as they walked along the narrow street where the music flared and argued with the sun.

'Apollo would have turned in his grave!' he remarked. 'Get in!'

They drove back to the hotel to collect Ariana's parcels from her shopping expedition earlier in the day, sitting on the terrace with a final drink of orange juice to watch the light change.

'I told your grandfather we might be late,' Nicolas said, 'and he agreed there was no need to hurry.'

A dish of long, juicy olives was brought to their table.

'Try some,' Ariana suggested. 'They are delicious.'

'You think of nothing but eating,' Nicolas teased her. 'If you are not careful you'll grow into a fat Greek matron with a double chin!'

'I've got several years left before that happens,' Ariana answered, helping herself to a plump olive as he passed round the dish.

He was his old charming self again, Rhea thought, teasing Ariana like a brother would and making sure that they were well entertained. The sombre, thoughtful man who had stood beside her on the terraces of the Marmaria was no longer in evidence, and the eyes which had looked into hers in the shadow of the Tholos were almost mocking now. A dark, painful colour stained her cheeks as she remembered his kiss and her own passionate response. What must he think of her?

Did it matter so very much? She looked away from the severely classical profile etched against the grandeur of the mountains, telling herself that it could only be a dream.

They stood up to go as the sun drew down towards the west, staining the cliffs a glowing red with its reflection while the whole ravine of the Pleistos and the steeply terraced vineyards in the valley were bathed in a deep purple light. Rhea held her breath, looking and looking until Nicolas touched her arm and they moved away.

It was quite dark by the time they reached Volponé, and the lanterns were lit along the terrace edge where John Karousis waited for their return. Rhea knew that she would always remember him sitting there under the vine pergola, smoking his pipe contentedly as he turned over the events of the day in his busy mind, and she wondered where he had been while they were at Delphi.

'You'll stay and take a meal with us,' he invited as Nicolas clasped his hand. 'Then you can tell me all that happened on Parnassos!'

Swiftly Rhea turned towards the open door of the kitchen where Evadne was supervising the evening meal.

'Can I help?' she offered automatically.

'It is all complete.' Her aunt indicated the lavishly-set table beyond her. 'Everything is ready for your return, even if we have now an extra guest.' She looked towards Nicolas and her father talking beneath the vines. 'You would be unwise to trust Nicolas Metaxas,' she warned. 'He is a man of many conquests, which you will discover to your cost.'

It was another douche of cold water thrown in her face by this embittered woman who would never try to like her, and because that final warning struck deep Rhea turned on her heel with the full intention of keeping Nicolas Metaxas at arm's length. Forcing herself to think back to her unhappy love affair of two years ago, she mounted the stairs to wash and change in the room next to her cousin's where Ariana was singing a melancholy love song.

During the elaborate meal Nicolas sat next to her, the same Nicolas but not quite the same. More than ever now she was conscious of his magnetism, of the way he looked and talked, and the way he used his hands. Their fingers had touched up there on the terraces of the Marmaria and he had held her strongly in his arms, but now he spoke only to his host and her gentle grandmother who frankly adored him. He was a charmer, Evadne had warned, and perhaps it was true.

When he rose to go he looked down at her earnestly.

'Will you come to the island?' he asked. 'You could help with the dig. It's what we do most weekends over there, and I'm sure you will find it interesting.'

'Why not?' she answered in her most off-hand manner. 'I understand it's the thing to do.'

He looked surprised.

'Not if you would prefer to go elsewhere,' he answered slowly. 'Talk to Ariana about it and let me know.'

He turned on his heel, leaving her where she stood under the mellow glow of the lantern, her eyes suddenly moist with tears.

For the remainder of the week they stayed at Volponé, helping where they could on the land, herding goats and weeding on the vine terraces where the grape harvest was beginning to form. It was an interesting new experience for Rhea and even Ariana did not seem to regret the loss of her car, but when it did arrive from the garage gleaming in its new coat of red enamel she immediately began to make plans.

'Nicolas has kept his word,' she declared, 'and now we must agree to help him. He needs as many people as he can get to work on the dig and we really ought to go. You must be interested when your father helped with the original excavations,' she added. 'Some Byzantine artefacts were discovered at the beginning of this year and Nicolas believes there are more.'

Evadne, who had been listening to their conversation as she sat with her embroidery on the terrace wall, looked across the sunlit flags to where Rhea stood in the shade.

'Your cousin may not wish to go,' she said to Ariana. 'She does not know the truth,' she added darkly.

Ariana jumped to her feet, scattering a basket of figs she had been preparing for their evening meal.

'Nicolas invited us!' she exclaimed. 'He has already asked us to go.'

Rhea went to sit beside her grandfather, who was smoking his pipe in the shadow of the wall.

'Can I ask you something?' she said. 'Something which seems to be almost personal. Nicolas Metaxas has asked me to go to Norbos at the weekend to help with the dig, but—there seems to be some sort of reason why I shouldn't, some fact or other that Aunt Evadne seems to think is important.'

John Karousis took his pipe from between his strong white teeth to study her for a moment in silence.

'Greece is full of facts and superstitions,' he said carefully. 'Do not listen to all you hear. There is no reason why you should not work for Nicolas on Norbos. Go and find out for yourself.'

It was the assurance she had needed, and she told Ariana she would go.

'Although I don't know the first thing about digging for ancient artefacts, or caring for them once they're found.'

'It is quite easy,' her cousin assured her. 'All you really need is care and a lot of patience. Anyway, it's much better than lying about in the sun hoping for a tan—much more satisfying.'

'I feel that it might be,' Rhea said. 'How do we get there—to Norbos?'

'Nicolas takes us across in his caique,' Ariana explained. 'He keeps it at Piraeus because he generally sails from there, but we can help by offering to make our own way to the port now that I have the Buggy back again.' Her loving gaze caressed the bright red bonnet as if the Renault had indeed been re-born. 'It's as good as new!'

'Certainly much better than it was at the beginning of the week?' Rhea laughed. 'We ought to tell Aunt Evadne our plans for the weekend right away, I think,' she added. 'I don't want her to feel that I'm taking her for granted.'

'She'd feel that anyway,' Ariana decided, glancing at her wristwatch. 'As long as Grandmama and 'Papa approve it doesn't much matter. We'll tell them when we come back.'

'Where are we going?' Rhea asked, following her swift progress along the terrace.

'Oh, hadn't I told you?' Ariana paused beside the sun-lounger Rhea had been using half an hour ago. 'We've just time for a swim at Florina. I brought your swimsuit down for you to save time.'

Rhea's blue swimsuit lay on the cane lounger, together with her towelling coat and a change of shoes.

'Do you think we should?' she asked with an odd feeling of reluctance. 'Perhaps we should wait till we're asked.'

'We could wait for ever in that case,' Ariana declared firmly. 'It's understood that we can use the pool whenever we like, and you said you enjoyed yourself the other day.'

'Perhaps it was different then,' Rhea heard herself saying.

'What do you mean?' Ariana turned to look at her. 'I can't see any difference, and Kyria Metaxas liked you.'

'She was being polite.'

'Anyway, you know Nicolas quite well now, so why are you so reluctant?'

'I don't know Nicolas at all,' Rhea said. 'He completely baffles me.'

'That's stupid, when he was so kind to us at Delphi!' Ariana pointed out.

Rhea did not want to speak about Delphi, to relive even for a moment the confusion she had felt when

Nicolas had kissed her and she had responded without hesitation to his swift embrace.

'Do you think he'll be at Florina?' she asked.

Ariana shook her head.

'No. He's generally busy in Athens at the end of the week, working to make up for the time he spends on the island. Usually we're there till Monday morning, but there are always a few people who stay over and work for a full week. We could do that later on, if you would like to,' she suggested.

Rhea picked up her swimsuit to follow her down the terrace steps.

'We'll see,' she said. 'I don't want Nicolas to feel that he's got to look after me because of his friendship with Grandpapa.'

When they reached Florina the pool in the garden was deserted, but there were canvas sun-beds on the terrace surrounding it, as if someone had recently been there.

'I'm going to be first in if you don't come out of that reverie you've been in since we left Volponé!' Ariana suggested. 'Why are you worrying so much when we've been here before? Kyria Metaxas would have told us if she didn't want us to come.'

Which was probably the truth, Rhea decided, following her to the little marble-fronted changing-room at the far side of the pool which was so like a Doric temple that the memory of the shattered Tholos came surging back to mock the rapid beating of her foolish heart.

'I'm ready!' Ariana cried. 'Bring your towelling coat and we'll sit on the terrace afterwards.'

They swam in the sheltered pool for almost an hour but still there was no sign of life on the steps leading up to the house or on the terrace surrounding it. The house itself looked curiously deserted, with only one window open at the front and a fine lace curtain wafting from another one on the balcony above.

'Kyria Metaxas won't be there,' Ariana remembered. 'She'll be in Athens, at the shop. The weekend is always a busy time for her, you understand.'

'It must be fun selling antiques and that sort of thing,' Rhea mused, lying down on one of the marble slabs which surrounded the pool and squinting up at the westering sun. 'Has she always done it?'

'For a long time.' Ariana sat down beside her, squeezing the water out of her hair. 'I think she needed very much to do something after Kyrie Metaxas died—not to just sit and mourn and wear black. She is a very clever person and it would have been a great waste of her talents, don't you think?'

'Was Nicolas very young when she was widowed?' Rhea asked almost involuntarily.

'He was twenty, but he was already in the family business,' Ariana informed her. 'He was suddenly a man.'

With all a man's responsibilities, Rhea thought, yet he managed to lead a very full life of his own.

'Does Kyria Metaxas go to Norbos?'

Ariana shrugged.

'Not very often. It's not the sort of thing she likes very much—digging in the sand.'

Ariana had said much the same sort of thing about Daphne, yet the two women were not alike. Rhea closed her eyes against the sun, feeling its comforting warmth on her skin like a caress until a shadow fell across her body and she sat bolt upright to find Nicolas Metaxas standing over them.

'The Mermaid brigade!' he said at his most provocative. 'May I sit down, or is it "ladies only" this afternoon?'

'*Nicos!*' Ariana protested, sitting up to hug her knees as she squinted up at him through the sunshine. 'You appear in the most unexpected places!'

'Why unexpected?' he countered mildly. 'This is my home.'

'But why are you here,' she demanded, 'in the middle of the afternoon?'

'I had some tools to collect and I was passing anyway. Have you enjoyed your swim?'

The question was directed at Rhea who sat up to answer him, her back very straight, her eyes deliberately on the expanse of sparkling blue water in the pool.

'We appreciate it very much,' she said. 'Especially as Volponé is so far from the sea.'

'Then come to the island,' he said. 'I'll take an extra trowel and a brush along for you, but you must bring your own prayer-mat.'

'I'm not sure what that means.' His offhand manner had matched her own.

'He means you have to find something to kneel on,' Ariana explained. 'A mat of some sort. I'll find one for you,' she offered.

'Do I take it as confirmed?' Nicolas asked. 'You've changed your mind about helping at the dig? The other day you were not at all sure.'

'Only because I thought I couldn't do the job properly,' Rhea told him. 'Now—everybody thinks I should help.'

'Including me!' He held out his hand to assist her to her feet. 'Will you come up to the house and have something to drink?' he asked. 'You can dry off as easily on the terrace as down here. Easier, as a matter of fact, because the last of the sun is still up there.'

She avoided his outstretched hand, scrambling to her feet unaided as Ariana had done because she could not risk even such a small contact while she was remembering Delphi and the intimate touch of his lips.

They climbed the weed-strewn steps to the terrace where the marble was cool under their bare feet and the sun glistened on their wet hair.

'My mother has gone back to Athens,' he explained, 'but I can still produce some tea. As a matter of fact, I'm quite good at it,' he boasted with a sudden smile. 'I've had a long apprenticeship.'

'On the caique,' Ariana supplied for Rhea's benefit. 'It's easier than percolating coffee when you're at sea.'

It seemed that she was no stranger to the caique nor to the island, for that matter, but Rhea could understand her enthusiasm and it was evident that Nicolas appreciated her willing help. So—what could he possibly have in common with Daphne, who was so unlike her younger cousin? Just that Daphne was beautiful and seductive, perhaps, and therefore desirable to a man like Nicolas.

A man like Nicolas? She found herself looking at him again and again as they sat in the sun, wondering about him, trying to fit the enigma of his personality into something she could understand, although he was evidently not going to help her. Blandly he served them tea when it was brought out to the terrace by Semele, playing host in his mother's absence with complete confidence while their hair dried in the sun.

'You will go back to Athens tomorrow,' Ariana suggested as they rose to leave.

'Unfortunately, yes.' He looked across the fertile valley at their feet. 'Otherwise I would have offered to drive you to Piraeus. I have a business meeting at eleven o'clock which also involves lunch, but no doubt I'll be free by three o'clock.'

'We'll go in early,' Ariana decided. 'Thank you for helping with the Buggy, Nicos. It's as good as new!'

'You're welcome!' He was looking down at her, veiling the amusement in his eyes. 'I have another surprise for you, by the way, but only if you manage to turn up promptly at Piraeus.'

'Tell me now!' demanded Ariana. 'I don't like delayed secrets. I like my surprises on the spot.'

'I'm well aware of that,' he agreed, 'but this surprise is rather special, as you will find out, and it's worth waiting for.'

'I can't imagine what it can be,' Ariana frowned. 'It isn't a new spade, or something equally unromantic?'

'Ochi!' he laughed, 'it isn't a new spade. It is something far more interesting and not so inanimate as a spade.'

'I wish you wouldn't talk in riddles,' Ariana objected. 'I shall lie awake all night now wondering what it is!'

'Not you!' he decided, helping Rhea on with her towelling coat. 'Even curiosity wouldn't keep you awake!'

He walked with them to the escarpment above the olive grove, as his mother had done, standing there in the last of the sunlight until they were out of sight among the trees, while Rhea walked back to Volponé fully aware now of his tremendous charm and her own deep response to it, although she decided to call it the reflection of the deep purple Grecian night.

'What,' she asked Ariana the following morning as they made beds together, 'are we supposed to wear while we dig?'

'Nothing fancy,' her cousin told her. 'We'll be working most of the time, but your swimsuit is a must, of course. Otherwise, it will be jeans and a T-shirt and perhaps a pretty dress for the evenings. Something quite simple, you understand, and no elaborate jewellery.'

'I had thought of taking my necklet,' Rhea said. 'It may be only a copy of the original, but it seems to belong there. What do you think?'

Ariana considered the question as she patted the last pillow into place.

'I don't think you should,' she decided at last. 'Even if it's only a copy it could be quite valuable and it will be heavy to wear. You could dress up your cotton with a pretty string of beads,' she advised. 'Once Daphne lost a valuable bracelet on Norbos and it caused a lot of trouble,' she added. 'Nicolas was very concerned about it, as you'll understand, and it quite spoilt the weekend for us all. He replaced it, of course, but it wasn't quite the same.'

'Then, beads it is!' Rhea agreed. 'What about my kneeling-mat?'

She felt happy and uplifted with a new experience to look forward to on this bright and sunny morning and her cousin's enthusiasm was infectious.

'I've found a mat for you,' Ariana assured her. 'You'll love it on the island,' she ran on. 'It's like no other place and the sea all round it is calm and beautiful in this weather. To sail in a caique will be a new experience for you and Nicolas would have been disappointed if you had refused to go. He really would like to be your friend.'

Rhea thought about Evadne's warning but decided to take her grandfather's advice not to listen to all she heard but to go and find out for herself.

'I've a feeling I'm going to enjoy myself,' she told

Ariana as they finally packed their canvas grips and went out to the car. 'It looks like a day for sailing.'

'*Kali andámosi!*' they called to the little group waving them goodbye from the terrace steps. 'See you on Monday!'

Their grandfather and grandmother were there and a visiting *papas* from the nearby village, but not Evadne. Their aunt had work to do.

They reached Piraeus in the early afternoon to find Nicolas waiting for them at one of the more attractive semi-circular basins which faced south towards Aegina. He was dressed casually in faded jeans and a cotton shirt, but nothing ever seemed to detract from the subtle air of authority which hedged him round.

'Everyone else is aboard,' he announced. 'I'll take your grips and you can park the Buggy at Gregory's.'

'Is he coming with us?' Ariana asked as she got back into the Renault. 'Perhaps not, when he's always so busy on a Friday.'

'Gregory owns one of the cafés over there,' Nicolas explained to Rhea, nodding towards the far side of the crescent-shaped waterfront. 'He won't be coming with us on this trip, but I have a good substitute, especially where Ariana is concerned.' Sudden laughter lines creased the corners of his eyes. 'It's my big surprise!'

'Someone she likes to be with,' Rhea guessed. 'Nicolas, you *do* tease her! She has spoken of little else all the way from Volponé. Is it really fair to treat her like a child?'

'Of course it is, because Ariana is still a little girl at heart,' he declared. 'Sophistication and the big world outside Volponé have passed her by.'

'We get on very well,' Rhea told him, supposing that he admired sophistication in a woman if he preferred Daphne to her younger cousin. 'Ariana is completely honest in everything she does.'

'I appreciate that,' he agreed lightly, leading the way towards a narrow jetty flanked by glistening white yachts of every size and description. 'My one hope for Ariana is that she'll never be hurt by falling in love with the wrong person. It can be disastrous.'

Rhea bit her lip as she felt the telltale colour of remembering staining her cheeks.

'I would wish her that, too,' she said quietly. 'The aftermath can last for a very long time.'

He looked down at her as if he would pose a question, thought better of it, and walked on.

'Are you a good sailor?' he asked.

'I don't really know,' she confessed. 'I've never been on a yacht before and certainly not a caique. Have they a bad reputation?'

'Not in this sort of weather,' he assured her, 'but they can be tricky in a storm.'

'Even in experienced hands?' She glanced at him sideways, smiling a little. 'I'm sure you must be an expert, although you don't wear a captain's hat.'

'I have one somewhere,' he said, drawing her eyes up to meet his amused gaze. 'I'll show it to you as soon as we go aboard.'

Before she could answer him in kind they had reached the last yacht in the line and a tall young man in white shorts and a blue T-shirt was coming down the gangplank towards them.

'Let me help,' he offered, taking one of the grips. 'Where's Ariana?'

'Parking the Buggy,' Nicolas informed him as he stepped aboard. 'Rhea, this is Michael Christos, who is a friend of Ariana.' He was smiling broadly. 'If she'd known he was on board she would have left me to park her car, I'm sure.'

Tall, fair and blue-eyed, Michael Christos was the very personification of the Marathon Youth with his boy's features and expression and the soft contours of his face which accentuated the gentle, dreamy expression of his eyes and mouth. Rhea had seen him so often depicted in marble or bronze, but here he was in the flesh, fair where Nicolas was dark, and somehow completely guileless, she thought. His fingers tightened momentarily over hers.

'I have heard much about you,' he said in English. 'We must show you as much as we can of Greece while you are here.'

'Michael!' The cry came from behind them as Ariana ran up the gangplank to kiss him on both cheeks. 'This must be Nicos's big surprise! When did you get home, and how did you get here?'

'Yesterday, and I flew in. I thought I had been away long enough.' He was answering her questions, one by one. 'And—yes, I suppose it must be a surprise!'

'Nicos should have told me.' Ariana stood back to admire him. 'You haven't changed at all.'

'Why should I have changed?' He began to walk along the deck with Ariana following at his heels like an obedient puppy. 'I always knew I would come back to Athens.'

Nicolas turned to Rhea, who was still waiting at the head of the gangplank.

'Welcome aboard!' he said. 'You'll have to accept me as your guide, since Ariana is otherwise employed.'

He was smiling again, glad that her cousin had been suitably surprised.

'I suppose they've known each other for a long time.' Rhea followed him along the white scrubbed deck. 'They look so right for each other.'

'They were at school together till Michael went to New York to the American branch of the family shipping company, but now he's back at Piraeus for good, I expect.'

'Will he help on your dig?' she asked.

'That's half the reason why he's here,' he said. 'Ariana is the other half. Michael is very keen on archaeology and at one time he thought of taking it up professionally, but the family business proved more demanding. His father needed someone in America and Michael went to New York to fill in a gap. Now it appears he has come home for good.'

'Into the bosom of his family,' Rhea mused. 'It's very Greek, isn't it?'

'I suppose so.' He paused at a sliding door which Michael and Ariana had left open for them. 'Down here,' he indicated. 'We're small, but there should be room for us all.'

He led the way down into a compact little saloon

with a mahogany table and two flanking benches which could be used as beds. There were four portholes, two on the jetty side and two where the sun streamed in over the water, rippling on the highly-polished mahogany like a glittering stream. Blue curtains with tiny yellow yachts on them were looped aside at each porthole and the covers on the benches were a matching yellow without the yachts.

'Daphne had a go at this,' he explained briefly. 'She thought there were enough small craft around, so she decided that the covers should be plain. At one time she toyed with doing interior decorating, but that fell through and she decided instead to model clothes and things.'

It was a man's vague sort of description of Daphne's ambitions which did not seem to interest him very much because, if she was to marry him, she would probably have to settle for the primary role of wife and mother.

They moved on through the cabin.

'This is the galley.' He pushed open a door. 'And in here is the captain's cabin which you can use for the crossing. For'ard there are two other cabins and cots for the crew, but these are rarely used. She isn't very big.'

'But she's your pride and joy,' Rhea guessed.

'My father bought her ten years ago when I was sixteen,' he said. 'She is one of the family now and never puts a foot wrong.' He deposited her grip in the captain's cabin. 'Feel at home,' he said.

Rhea looked about her. The cabin was neat and tidy—'ship shape and Bristol fashion', she thought, although that was perhaps a too-English term to apply to a Greek caique. There was a desk and a chart-table in one corner, and a narrow bunk covered in the same yellow corded cloth as the settees in the saloon, and yellow curtains printed with the little yachts hung on either side of the single porthole. She looked through it at the sea, momentarily dazzled by its brightness as Ariana came to claim her.

'On deck!' she commanded. 'We're ready to sail and everybody has to help.'

Nicolas was in the wheelhouse when they went up, while Michael stood ready to cast off. It was a magical moment for Rhea as they moved smoothly out of the bay and the sails were set. Nicolas switched off the engine and, dramatically, there was no more sound. It was a moment which brought them amazingly close— no sound, no contact with the land, just the smooth and gentle movement forward with the wind.

Nicolas passed her a chart so that she could plot their course along the coast, although she was quite sure that he must know it by heart.

'We're going south at the moment,' he told her, 'but soon we'll round Sounion and go east.'

She found the Cyclades on the chart, a scattering of many islands lying on a wide sea, and her heart began to beat hard and fast in her breast as she thought about their destination. Her father must have come to Norbos many times, as they were doing now, sailing smoothly along the coast past headlands and little harbours crowded with fish restaurants and sailing craft, past the airport and the smart beaches and nightclubs of Glifáda where the foothills of Hymettus came down to the sea. Pine-clad promontories with their villas and beaches and red rocks skirted the shore as they sailed before the gentle wind, while inland she could see rolling vineyards slumbering in the afternoon heat.

A wide corniche wound along the shore, in and out of little secret coves fringed with islets until, suddenly, the rocky promontory of Sounion rose above the dramatic sweep of a bay with the ruined temple of Poseidon crowning its cliff.

'Well,' Nicolas asked at her elbow, 'what do you think?'

They were alone because Ariana and Michael had scrambled along the deck to a vantage point for'ard where they could lie to look down at the bow wave cleaving the sun-dazzled water below.

'I can't,' she confessed. 'I can't think about anything but being here.'

If she had added 'with you' it might not have been so very far from the truth.

'Wait till you see Norbos,' he said.

Almost immediately they were in among the islands with the sun low over the mountains behind them and a bronze colour already settling on the sea. Norbos was no more than a speck on the chart when he pointed it out to her.

'It isn't very big, but it has everything, or so I like to think. I'm trying to build up a small local museum on the spot, things we've dug up at the excavations in recent years and some of the older artefacts which were original finds. There's one in particular,' he added, frowning, 'a Byzantine torque which disappeared some years ago. It could be the centrepiece of our collection, but I can't trace it.'

Rhea's thoughts went immediately to the necklet which had been her father's most treasured possession.

'What was it like?' she asked as Norbos came into view.

'The usual neck ornament—gold studded with semi-precious stones. You must have seen them in books or the copies made of them which are for sale in most of the shops.'

A choking sensation rose in Rhea's throat, but what she was thinking was ridiculous. Her necklet was only a copy of the original, she assured herself. Her father had told her so. How, then, could it possibly be the stolen artefact?

'I have a Byzantine necklet,' she confessed. 'It's only a copy, of course, but it is very beautiful.'

'You must show it to me,' he suggested.

'I haven't brought it with me. It—didn't seem appropriate to dress up and it's quite heavy to wear,' she explained.

Now that they were approaching the island Ariana was full of excitement as she ran towards them along the deck. 'There it is!' she said to Rhea. 'The most beautiful island in the whole Aegean!'

It was indeed beautiful. Small and no more than a speck on the ocean chart, its curved, sandy bays could be seen from a considerable distance, while the central peak of its rocky backbone stood out clearly against the sky, and Rhea was suddenly aware of a mounting excitement as they drew near. It was here, perhaps, that her father and mother had first met.

Nicolas came to stand beside her and she felt his compelling nearness once again.

'Did my mother come here?' she asked.

He shaded his eyes to look towards the shore.

'Many times, I believe,' he answered, his gaze settling on the remote peak which seemed to dominate the whole island.

They were sailing close to the shore and within minutes they had turned into a tiny, land-locked harbour where little white-washed houses climbed steeply from the shore and a fishing fleet of three sturdy boats lay along the mole. Two old men and several sun-bronzed boys were mending nets on the warm stone and they rushed to catch their mooring-ropes as Michael and Ariana let down the sails. There was a short exchange in Greek between Nicolas and the older men which must have had something to do with fish, because their catch of mullet and lobster was displayed immediately for their inspection amid happy smiles.

Nicolas helped Rhea ashore.

'Come and choose your supper,' he invited.

Michael stowed the sails while Ariana dived below decks for their luggage.

'I ought to help,' Rhea said.

'Supper is much more important.' Nicolas led her towards the fishing boats. 'Can you cook?' he asked.

'I'm quite good with fish, but I don't know about lobster,' she confessed. 'I don't like things wriggling round in the bottom of a boat waiting to be killed.'

He laughed, pointing to the mullet which was delivered to him in a rough string bag together with what seemed to be much advice in his native tongue.

'What did they say?' she asked as they walked along the mole. 'But perhaps you'd rather not tell me if it was a reflection on my culinary skill.'

'It wasn't that,' he assured her, smiling broadly. 'It was far more personal, as a matter of fact. They wondered if I had brought the right bride to Norbos at last.'

Coolly he looked at her, watching the hot colour of embarrassment mounting to her cheeks as she tried to avoid his eyes.

'Don't be too upset about it,' he added cheerfully. 'It's typically Greek. They are forever looking for romance, and curiosity is second nature to them.'

'They must know you very well. Are you always landing on Norbos with a prospective bride in tow?' Rhea asked.

'Hardly,' he smiled, 'but they're generally hopeful. They believe you should marry in your early twenties to provide sufficient heirs for the future. A young bride is essential to their way of thinking. Stratis—the one with the blue cap—has five sons and plenty of daughters to take care of him in his old age. The boys all work for him on the boats and even the youngest learns how to mend nets long before he goes out to fish.'

Before they had turned away he had shaken hands with the two fishermen who had raised their caps respectfully in Rhea's direction.

'You've impressed them,' he said. 'They like to know who's who.'

It was obvious that he was deeply respected quite apart from the fact that he owned the island where they made a living and where they had probably been born. No doubt he was the final authority and they knew he would be fair.

Ariana was laughing when she finally rejoined them at the end of the mole.

'Nicolas has brought so much stuff over with him that we won't be able to use the cart,' she said. 'You'll have to ride a mule!'

It appeared that there was no transport on Norbos apart from a large-wheeled cart and several mules which the fishermen were already helping to load with their belongings and several packages for the dig.

'Better ride,' Nicolas advised, seeing her hesitation. 'It's more than a mile and our roads are rough.' He selected a docile-looking animal from the waiting line of *moulári* for her closer inspection. 'This one ought to be all right, and you'll be led. There's really nothing to it.'

He stood waiting, and then he put his hands on her waist to lift her into the saddle. She looked down at him and was suddenly overwhelmed by the sense of immense power in him, and in those magnetic blue eyes, as her heart began to beat strongly in her breast. It seemed an eternity before she could look away.

Ariana's mount was stubborn, causing much laughter as they tried to persuade it up the steep, narrow street between the houses which was the only way out of the tiny port. The two men walked on either side of the mules, prodding them when necessary, while the cart trundled along behind, drawn by two grey mules with the longest ears Rhea had ever seen. Her own mount seemed completely unconscious of her weight, plodding on and up with a stoic indifference to everything about him and Michael's stick in particular.

Out of his conventional city attire Nicolas seemed a different being, his cotton shirt open to the waist now, his jeans stained with sea water and his feet still thrust into the comfortable white *espadrilles* which had seen a lot of wear.

Their destination was a large white house on a hill surrounded by trees, and nearby there was another villa where the people helping at the excavations were accommodated from time to time. There seemed to be little else on the uplands except a white-washed cottage or two surrounded by patch-work fields where meagre crops of barley were grown. Vine terraces scarred the hillsides here and there, leading up to the crenellated walls of a ruined fortress which had originally guarded the harbour but was now crumbling where it stood. Yet, like most other ancient forts in Greece, it dominated the skyline as the last rays of the sun found it to set the mellow stone on fire.

They reached the villa, passed it and went on to the square white house on the hill. It was larger than Rhea had thought at first, with dark blue shutters at the windows and a garden enclosed by a white stone wall. The whiteness of everything in Greece had astonished her: white-washed cubist houses; white temples standing out against the incredible blue of a cloudless sky; white sanded beaches hugging the shore and white marble terraces glittering in the sun.

Here on Norbos it was the same, with the white sails of little yachts dotting the turquoise sea between the islands and a long white cloud hovering above the high, square backbone of Andros like a pennant in the wind.

Nicolas halted the mules and one of the men rushed forward to open the blue-painted gates in the white wall. Through them Rhea made out a lovely old courtyard smothered in flowers and a sheltering pergola where roses grew in profusion among the overhanging vines. A white, towered dovecot stood in the centre attracting butterflies as well as doves. It was the loveliest place she had ever seen, with big terracotta urns spilling colour over the steps, and beds of petunias and geraniums bordering an ancient mosaic pavement which formed the entrance to the house itself. White lace curtains hung outside the windows where an errant breeze had flicked them across the sill earlier in the day, and the blue painted door stood invitingly open.

A small, stout woman in a black, lavishly-embroidered skirt and white blouse came to meet them.

'This is Kyria Kotsovos who looks after us all,' Nicolas explained. 'She'll make sure of your comfort and see that you get up in the morning in good time!'

The housekeeper beamed as he handed her a bulky package, a gift he had brought for her from Athens, thanking him in rapid Greek as she clasped it to her ample bosom.

'Everyone is Nicos's slave,' Ariana remarked, leading the way into the house across the polished wood floor of a wide hall spread with beautiful Persian rugs. 'He charms even the island people, as you see!'

They mounted a narrow staircase which climbed to the upper storey between white-painted walls where light flooded in through high, arched windows, a pink light dyed by the departing sun.

'We'll be sharing a room,' Ariana told her. 'Just in case Nicolas has other guests who are rather special. Normally we stay at the lodge which we passed on the way up, or in the *hora* if things get really crowded during the summer. The village women are always eager to have visitors staying with them, you understand. They do not see many people here because the island has never been a tourist attraction like Delos or Míkanos with their splendid beaches and modern hotels.'

A door stood open at the head of the stairs and she led the way in.

'Here we are!' she announced. 'Everything has been prepared.'

There were two identical beds with carved head-boards, two dressing-chests, a large wardrobe, and hand-woven rugs on the polished floor. White lace curtains hung at the double window opening on to a little balcony, and there was an adjoining bathroom with a shower.

'This is the grandest room,' her cousin informed her. 'It's mostly kept for family.'

Rhea turned back from the open window where she had been admiring the view.

'What about Nicolas?' she asked. 'Doesn't he use it?'

'Oh, no. He sleeps across the garden in a place of his own. It was an old outhouse, and he converted it to suit himself when he comes to Norbos in the winter so that he needn't open up the whole house for one person.'

They showered and changed into skirts and blouses as night took over in the garden below and Rhea stepped out on to the balcony to watch for the stars.

Was it here that her mother and father had met and loved? Was it here that Maria Karousis had struggled with her loyalty to her family and her native land, sacrificing both in the end to return to England with a stranger? The man she loved! It had an awesome sound about it, defeating all argument, all regret and she must have been very sure of that love when she had made her decision. Rhea knew that her parents had been very happy together, but it was only now that she realised how her mother must have felt, torn between those two great passions and saddened by the hurt she must have inflicted on the man she had been going to marry.

Nicolas's father! He must have paced these quiet terraces in angry defeat and bitter resentment, upbraiding his friend and the woman who had promised to be his wife. Yet he had married soon afterwards, because Nicolas was twenty-six. She knew that five long years had passed before she was born, but that might have been an adjustment period for her mother in a strange land.

A bell sounded through the quiet house.

'Time to go down,' Ariana said. 'We eat early because we are always ready to tumble into bed after a day out on the dig, and because Kyria Kotsovos must cook for her own family when she returns to the *hora*.'

They sat under the vine pergola till the meal was announced, sipping orange juice while the men drank their small glasses of *ouzo*. Michael had graced the occasion by donning tight white trousers and a colourful red cummerbund into which he had tucked a full-sleeved tunic, and Nicolas had changed into conventional slacks with a blue cravat knotted at the neck of his cotton shirt.

Very soon the appetising aroma of lamb being cooked on a spit permeated the scented air and Nicolas got up to lead the way to a covered terrace at the back of the house where their meal was waiting. They ate heartily, laughing and talking eagerly about the possible finds they might make the following day at the dig and those discovered in the past.

'Rhea has a necklet that's supposed to be a copy of the torque found at the *hora* a long time ago,' Ariana explained to Michael. 'She should have brought it with her and worn it tonight, because you're all dressed up!'

'I didn't think it was quite the occasion,' Rhea said, 'though I suppose it does belong here, even if it is only a copy.' She was suddenly aware of Nicolas looking intently in her direction. 'I suppose I feel that I don't really suit anything quite so grand,' she added lamely.

'You're half Greek,' Ariana pointed out, 'so why should you not wear it? Daphne wears that sort of jewellery all the time,' she added, 'more because it's terribly dramatic and suits her than because she wants to be Greek.'

'Daphne and Rhea don't look at all alike,' Michael decided as Nicolas got up to fill their glasses with wine. 'I'd say they were poles apart, even although they are cousins.'

Rhea was aware of Nicolas standing behind her, not adding anything to the conversation for the first time, and she wondered if he resented the implied criticism in Michael's careless words.

'Are you going to try our *retsina*?' Michael asked gaily. 'I must warn you that it tastes like turpentine when you aren't used to drinking it!'

'I'm offering Rhea an alternative,' Nicolas said at last. 'We can't expect her to accept everything Greek after only a day or two.' He bent over the table with two bottles in his hand. 'Your choice,' he said.

Rhea met his eyes above the flickering lamplight.

'I'm going Greek,' she laughed. 'I'll try the *retsina* and be brave about it!'

'It will be a change from orange juice,' he allowed, pouring the strangely resinated wine into her glass, 'but if you don't like it feel free to change your mind.'

The meal passed quickly. Kyria Kotsovos was an excellent cook and had done her best to please them.

'Do we eat like this every day?' Rhea asked, settling down again under the vine pergola to enjoy a cup of excellent Turkish coffee as Michael picked up the guitar he had left beside his chair and began to play. 'If so, I don't think we'll get much work done.'

'This is an incentive,' Nicolas admitted, sitting down beside her. 'If you don't work tomorrow you don't eat!'

The song Michael chose was a love song, erotic and softly persuasive as it stole across the scented air, rising through the tracery of vine leaves into the warm, dark night above. It was meant for Ariana, but the poignant melody reached deep into Rhea's heart till she thought that she could listen to it for ever. It held all of Greece for her, its mystery and its melancholy and the deep, deep longing she had come to recognise in her heart.

Michael played for over an hour while Ariana sang

the words of the songs in a sweet, clear soprano, haunting the night with its beauty as the stars grew brighter and a fledgling moon rose above the mountain rim to look at them.

Nicolas seemed content, sitting in a long cane chair at the terrace edge, his hands clasped idly across his chest as he planned for tomorrow.

'We'll go straight up to the excavations,' he decided. 'I'd like to uncover the rest of the north-east corner, if possible, before we think of opening the museum even with the few artefacts we have ready. It's not just a task for a day, but at least the walls will be exposed.' He looked across the terrace to where Ariana sat on a low marble bench at the musician's side. 'Are you still offering to do the cataloguing?' he asked.

'Yes, I promised,' Ariana assured him. 'I will keep my word and—Rhea could help also.'

There was the briefest pause before Nicolas answered.

'That will be up to Rhea and how she feels about working on a holiday,' he said.

Michael rose to his feet.

'Time to go down,' he said. 'I'll see you in the morning—early!'

He went away, playing his guitar, not a love song this time but a stirring march as he covered the distance between the house and the villa where he lodged. He had become wholly natural, wholly Greek, the veneer of the New World sophistication he had acquired in New York completely gone. They stood watching until the last of his music faded in the distance, and then Ariana said with a yawn,

'I'm off to bed. Don't wait up too long!'

Rhea stood looking out over the silent garden and the terraces towards the sea, feeling the beauty of the scented night like some tangible thing as Nicholas stood beside her smoking a small cheroot.

'Will you help with the cataloguing?' he asked presently. 'Ariana will show you how to do it.'

'I'd love to.' She turned towards him. 'I'm looking forward to tomorrow and working on the dig.'

He smiled faintly as he turned away.

'I wonder if you'll repeat that after tomorrow,' he said. 'You'll ache in all the muscles you didn't know you had!'

'I'll risk it, Nicolas.' She walked with him to the terrace steps. 'Good night.'

'*Kalinikta!*' he said gently. 'Sleep well!'

CHAPTER FOUR

THE sun was pouring in through the lace curtains of their bedroom when Ariana wakened her the following morning.

'Time to go to work!' she called, splashing cold water on to her face in the bathroom beyond. 'It's a matter of principle not to be late.'

They breakfasted on the terrace on croissants, fruit juice and coffee, followed by a large slice of honey cake which Kyria Kotsovos had baked for them, and soon they were on their way down the hillside with the early morning sun warm on their faces and quite a lot of excitement in their hearts.

'I'd no idea Michael would be here,' Ariana confessed, blushing a little. 'I thought he had gone to New York for good.'

'He's older than you are,' Rhea reflected.

'Only a little bit older. Four years, to be exact. He used to carry my books to school for me, but everything seemed to be over when he went to America,' Ariana sighed.

'Everything?' Rhea stole a look at her cousin's flushed face.

'We were in love with each other, like Orpheus and Euridice,' Ariana declared. 'We held hands and walked through the fields together among the flowers.'

'And now he has come back,' Rhea said. 'You must be very happy.'

'Certainly I am, so long as he stays in Athens and doesn't go away again,' Ariana sighed, brightening to add, 'but that is a thought for tomorrow. Now we can laugh and be happy all day long!'

Nicholas must have gone on ahead of them because the road they had travelled the previous afternoon was deserted. They could see the tiny port and the white houses of the *hora* far beneath them and the gleam of a large white yacht sailing past.

'Does Nicolas often have visitors?' Rhea asked.

'Not on a yacht like that one,' Ariana declared. 'People like that wouldn't know what to do on a dig. They'd get their hands dirty!'

They branched off on to a rough track leading across a plateau where a ruined Frankish tower looked out over the sea, and here, in the shelter of a high limestone cliff, Nicolas had begun his search. Some of the excavations dated from his father's time, but he had extended them eastwards to uncover some lovely mosaic pavements which he was eager to restore.

Several other people were already at work on the pavements and they could see Nicolas filling the water tank at the end of the site. When they went towards him he looked up with a smile.

'I thought it a shame to disturb you at seven o'clock,' he said, handing Rhea a trowel and the little brush she would most certainly need. 'Ariana will show you how to use them and I'll bring you a bucket in a moment or two.'

Rhea had no idea how fascinating it would prove to be. She sat in the sun with the linen hat Nicolas had insisted on pulled well forward on her head, scraping carefully and brushing away the dust over a hard surface, and scraping again to uncover little more than a scrap of colourful pottery for her morning's work. She was washing it when Nicolas came back to stand beside her.

'Well, what do you think?' he asked. 'Are you ready to give up and call it a day?'

She took her hat off to look at him, aware that they were both hot and dishevelled—but satisfied.

'I'm beginning to realise what it's all about,' she said. 'The impetus of the whole thing that drives you on.' She looked down at the broken piece of pottery in her hand. 'When I saw the design and all those lovely colours coming up under the water I knew what it must be like to make an important find.'

He took the piece of pottery from her, examining it carefully in the bright, clear light.

'It's quite ordinary,' he said. 'Part of an old jug that

could have been used in the kitchen, but that doesn't mean it isn't interesting in itself.' He looked towards the far side of the excavations. 'George will date it for us later. Meanwhile, come and have something to eat. It's past twelve o'clock.'

She had been working steadily for three hours and had scarcely noticed the passage of time.

They ate a packed lunch in the shadow of the tower, leaning back against the ancient stone while they gazed out towards the surrounding islands lying like anchored ships on a tranquil sea. Norbos must have been the smallest of them all, a mere pin-prick on the turquoise water, a satellite island which had probably been the peak of a volcano in the distant past, but was now green and fertile like most of the others. It was a time to linger and look and speculate; a time filled with contentment and the desire to stay here for ever.

'You won't have to work all the time,' Nicolas told her. 'We also know how to play. George has brought his sail-plane over and we will also teach you to water-ski.'

'I don't know whether I'm brave enough,' Rhea laughed. 'I'd find ski-ing difficult on dry land, I expect, though I've never tried it.'

They were sitting round in a group, talking in the desultory fashion of strangers with an interest in common, and very soon she felt accepted in spite of the fact that she had no real knowledge to offer them. At three o'clock Michael glanced at his watch.

'We can put in another two hours,' he suggested, 'now that it's not so hot. Then I'll challenge all comers to a race in the bay!'

Rhea got stiffly to her feet, remembering what Nicolas had said about cramped muscles after crouching too long in one position.

'I'll kneel, for a change,' she decided, taking up her mat when they returned to the spot where they had been working all morning.

'You've got a lovely streak of mud down one side of your face,' Ariana informed her, taking up a brush.

Rhea shrugged.

'It will rub off. I never could work tidily.' She pulled the linen hat down on her brow. 'We all look much in need of a shower, I guess.'

Michael stood above them, looking down towards the *hora* and the white mole stretching into the sea.

'There's a yacht coming in,' he said. 'The big launch that was cruising round this morning, but it doesn't look like an influx of helpers,' he decided, jumping down beside them from the surrounding wall. 'Too big and too posh!'

People were coming ashore, tiny specks too far away for recognition as they crossed the gangway to the sun-washed stone of the mole.

'I suppose they have a right,' Ariana mused, 'but they generally hold us up asking stupid questions and tramping over everything we've just dusted, like the pavements, for instance.'

Rhea knelt on her mat, scraping carefully with her trowel where she had left off while Nicolas crossed to the far end of the site to inspect a find by one of the students who had been there for the past few days. Nothing of great importance had been unearthed for over a month and he was eager to see what had been found.

Ariana moved further along the exposed pavement, brushing diligently, while Rhea continued to scrape and brush, piling up a small mound of earth which she would sieve carefully when she had enough. It was still very warm, and once or twice she passed the back of her hand across her forehead to sweep aside her hair, feeling that a shower would not come amiss at the ending of the day.

Absorbed in her task, she was unaware of being overlooked until a long shadow fell across her shoulders on to the area of soil where she was working.

'You're having a lovely time wallowing in the dust!'

The voice was coolly amused, and she looked up to find the tall, immaculate girl she had first seen with Nicolas at the airport looking down at her. It was her cousin Daphne.

'You must be Rhea,' Daphne said. 'Are you enjoying yourself?'

Feeling dusty and dishevelled in the face of so much perfection, Rhea struggled to her feet.

'I had no idea we would meet like this,' she confessed because she couldn't think of anything better to say in the circumstances. 'I—thought you were in Rome.'

Daphne laughed, showing splendid teeth between painted lips which looked slightly inappropriate in the bright afternoon sunshine.

'I was—until yesterday,' she said. 'Then I had a chance to fly back to Athens privately and come on here.' She looked down towards the harbour. 'We're on a cruise,' she explained, 'but I couldn't resist coming ashore to check up on Nicolas and his amazing goings-on.'

Ariana came across from the other side of the wall.

'I might have known it was you,' she said ungraciously as she recognised her cousin, 'and I don't suppose you've come to work.'

Daphne looked shocked at the idea.

'Work?' she repeated. 'If you mean grubbing around in the mud looking for bits of broken jugs—no! I have more to do with my time.' She looked straight at Rhea as she turned to cross the pavement to the far side of the excavations where Nicolas was talking earnestly to one of the students. 'I didn't know you were an archaeologist,' she said coldly.

'A very modest amateur,' Rhea answered, 'but I'm beginning to learn.'

Daphne picked her delicate way between the mosaics, hardly noticing them in her determined search for Nicolas.

'I wonder why she came,' Ariana said bleakly. 'What can she possibly want on Nicolas's island?'

'She may feel she has every right to be here,' Rhea suggested, digging carelessly. 'If she's going to marry Nicolas——'

'She *intends* to marry him, if nothing better turns up!' Ariana picked up her trowel, going back to work along the wall. 'I hope she doesn't stay.'

It looked very much as if Daphne intended to stay, at

least over the weekend. She stood beside Nicolas in her immaculate white trousers and pink silk shirt inspecting the progress he had made as if she were really interested in his work, trying not to show her boredom and walking with him along the length of the excavated wall when he decided it was time to finish for the day.

'Come down to the yacht and meet the rest of our party,' she invited when they halted just short of where Rhea was washing the last of her finds. 'I think you already know Philip and Ida Xilas. Their son, Paris, is with them, and Jason Papadam.'

Rhea heard Nicolas excusing himself, saying he was in no fit state to go aboard an immaculate yacht.

'Besides,' he added, 'Mama Kotsovos will have a meal prepared for us when we go back and we can't disappoint her.'

'You allow her too much freedom,' Daphne accused him. 'She runs the house as if it was her own.'

'I have to rely on her services,' Nicolas pointed out, 'and she is exceedingly loyal.' He turned to Rhea. 'Time to stop work and come back to the house,' he said. 'You've done enough for your first day.'

He walked off to summon the others as Rhea collected her tools.

'I thought you would have been staying at the Lodge,' Daphne said, frowning. 'Ariana generally sleeps there with the other workers.'

'It's quite different this time.' It seemed to Rhea that her younger cousin had come to her rescue. 'We are Nicos's special guests,' Ariana added wilfully.

'Well, now, that certainly *is* something,' Daphne observed drily. 'Since when, may I ask, have you qualified for such important treatment?'

'Since Rhea arrived, I suppose,' Ariana returned pointedly. 'Nicolas is very grateful for her help.'

Daphne laughed.

'That I *can* believe.' She looked pointedly at Rhea. 'Nicolas expects everyone to work for their keep when they come to Norbos, but I have no intention of digging my fingernails away. How long do you intend to stay?' she asked.

'On Norbos? Just for the weekend,' Rhea answered.

'I meant in Greece,' Daphne said. 'At Volponé.'

It was the question her mother had asked in almost the same tone of voice, but this time it didn't seem to hurt so much. Rhea drew a deep breath.

'At least for a month,' she said. 'Grandpapa and Grandmama have made me welcome.'

Daphne appeared to be amused.

'You'll soon get tired of it—after London,' she predicted. 'Volponé isn't exactly Athens, either.'

'I think it's beautiful,' Rhea declared.

'And dull.' Daphne tucked the silk blouse more securely into her belt. 'I must go, but I'll see you later. It looks very much as if the yacht will be moored here for the rest of the weekend.'

She wandered off in Nicolas's direction, linking her arm in his when they met to show how intimate they were.

'She'll turn up and spoil the evening for us,' Ariana grumbled as they walked back to the house. 'Daphne's like that. She's very jealous of her conquests.'

'She may have a conquest on board the yacht,' Rhea suggested.

'In that case, she'll leave him behind.' Ariana swung her bucket as they climbed back up the hill. 'She wouldn't want Nicolas to meet him.'

Nicolas had called in at the Lodge, but he overtook them as they reached the gates.

'Michael is invited to dinner,' he informed them. 'He will come up as soon as he's changed and we can have some more music.'

'Nicos, you think of everything!' Ariana smiled. 'Did you tell him to bring his guitar?'

'He never goes anywhere without it,' Nicolas said. 'Are you tired?' He directed the question to Rhea as he opened the gates to let them through. 'It's the logical reaction after a first day on a dig.'

'A shower will work wonders,' Rhea assured him, 'and I'm looking forward to a meal. I've enjoyed today, Nicolas, very much,' she added as they crossed the courtyard. 'It was fascinating.'

'We'll make an archaeologist out of you yet!' He

paused at the end of the terrace where the steps went down to his own domain. 'See you at eight o'clock!'

'He'll start on some paper work,' Ariana guessed. 'There is a lot to do before we begin the actual cataloguing, you understand.'

When they had washed and changed into their skirts and clean blouses they sat on the terrace watching the sun set beyond the mountain rim to throw back a flame of colour until the purple shadows took over and the night came into its own.

Ariana looked content as they listened to the drowsy cooing from the dovecote and the whisper of the night wind as it rustled the leaves. Nicolas came upon them suddenly.

'I thought we might have an *aperitif*,' he suggested. 'What would you like? Sherry or *ouzo*, if you have come to like it?'

Rhea returned his smile.

'Sherry, please,' she said. 'I haven't quite got the hang of *ouzo* yet.'

'You stand condemned!' he told her. 'Ariana?'

'I'll have some sherry. I don't like *ouzo* either.'

'You're hard to please.' He walked towards the house. 'Michael will be here any minute.'

The gate creaked as it was opened and Michael made his appearance, complete with guitar.

'The others are coming over after they've eaten,' he announced. 'They enjoy a sing-song.'

Kyria Kotsovos served their meal on the terrace at the back of the house and immediately afterwards four of the students who had helped on the excavations all day arrived to sing the remainder of the evening away in typical Grecian abandonment.

'One glass of *ouzo* brings the necessary sparkle to their eyes,' Michael said. 'They don't *have* to be tanked up to enjoy themselves.'

The occasional Americanism slipped out when it was least expected, Rhea thought, and it made him more attractive than ever. He was so right for Ariana that it was difficult to fault him as he strummed lazily on his guitar, gazing up at her in the moonlight.

When the gate creaked a second time they all turned to peer across the lamplit courtyard to where a little cluster of torches wavered like uncertain fireflies against the dark foliage of the oleanders.'

'Someone's coming,' Ariana said dolefully. 'It must be Daphne.'

Their cousin came forward with the rest of her companions from the yacht. They had walked up in the moonlight, carrying torches for a surer footing on the rough road, and even Daphne wore sensible shoes.

'Surprise! Surprise!' she cried when Nicolas rose to greet her. 'We had nothing to do and Jason wanted to meet you.' She paused under one of the lanterns to introduce her host and hostess. 'You know Philip and Ida, of course, and Paris, but I don't think you've met Jason Papadam. He's from Corinth originally.' Her dark eyes glittered in the artificial light as she looked across the terrace at Nicolas's other guests. 'You're having quite a party,' she decided.

She had made no attempt to introduce Rhea, but it seemed that Jason Papadam was hardly a conquest when she had brought him to meet Nicolas. Remembering her conversation with Ariana such a short time ago, Rhea felt that their evening sing-song had been completely spoiled.

Daphne wore a white silk shawl over a dramatic emerald-green dress and she changed her walking shoes for a pair of matching high-heeled sandals which she had brought with her in a linen shoulder-bag.

'I can't bear dowdy footwear,' she announced, looking around for the necessary admiration.

'A drink?' Nicolas suggested when he had welcomed his other guests.

'Darling Nicos!' Daphne laughed. 'How clever of you! We're simply parched after that long climb. It must be at least three miles from the *hora* to here.'

'One mile exactly,' Nicolas informed her, going back to the house to bring the wine.

'Can I help?' Daphne called after him. 'I know my way about.'

Ariana jumped to her feet.

'I can do it,' she said. 'You're a guest, Daphne.'

Michael ran tentative fingers over the strings of his guitar, strumming softly.

'I thought you were in America.' Daphne sat down beside him. 'Last time I heard you were on your way to New York.'

'That was two years ago,' Michael reminded her. 'I'm back now.'

'And likely to stay?'

'I guess so.'

'Are you sleeping here, in the house?' she asked.

'At the Lodge.' He put the guitar aside. 'We're here to work on the excavations.'

'So I noticed. Are you genuinely interested, or is it all just fun?'

'A bit of both. No one could be with Nicolas for long without becoming interested in what he's attempting to do.'

'True,' she allowed. 'But—all that grubbing about in the earth!' She looked up as Ariana and Nicolas reappeared with a tray of glasses and the wine. 'I'll do your cataloguing for you, Nicolas,' she offered. 'I'm rather good at it, remember?'

Nicolas put the tray down on the terrace wall.

'I've already asked Ariana,' he said.

'And Rhea!' Ariana was quick to add. 'Two helpers are quite enough, and it will take longer than one weekend.'

Daphne's smile was suddenly remote.

'We must go into that,' she said, glancing in Nicolas's direction as he poured the wine.

As the party progressed Rhea attempted to forget her older cousin and enjoy herself. Daphne appeared to be deliberately antagonistic, but she would not allow her to spoil this ideal evening of song and companionship under the Aegean stars. The night was magical and when Nicolas finally came to sit beside her all seemed to be well.

'Are you serious about helping Ariana with the cataloguing?' he asked. 'It would save me a lot of time.'

'I'll be glad to do it,' she told him firmly. 'It will be—

a sort of tribute to my father's memory,' she added huskily.

When Michael started to play again some of the students got up to dance and she was swept into the stream of gaiety, a willing pupil, while Nicolas stood aside to watch. Daphne danced once with Jason Papadam and again with Paris, a tall, angular youth very like his mother, and then she sat down on the terrace wall to monopolise their host for the remainder of the evening. Whatever she had to say to Nicolas, she appeared to be very earnest about it, and when the Xilas family rose to go she had obviously made arrangements for the following day.

'Philip and Ida will want to go to church in the morning,' Rhea heard her saying to Nicolas, 'but you can come down any time after that and we're sure to be on board. You needn't worry about dressing because we're all coming back to help on your dig afterwards. Philip is quite curious about it and Ida will go anywhere to please him, as you know. Paris has decided to water-ski and I think Jason will go with him,' she added briefly. 'Anyway, he can please himself.'

Michael came to stand beside Rhea as the rest of the party said good night.

'I don't suppose they could accommodate us all on the yacht,' he mused, 'even if it is half the size of the *QE II*. Were you invited?'

'I don't think so. Perhaps Daphne didn't consider it necessary—being family,' Rhea smiled. 'I don't think Ariana is invited, either.'

'Fair enough!' he said. 'We'll go snorkelling instead.'

'What about the "dig"?'

'We don't work on a Sunday morning,' he said. 'It's always been a house rule and Daphne was well aware of it when she arranged her little sherry party on board Philip's yacht. She exploits people all the time, using them for her own advantage—or hadn't you noticed?'

'I noticed,' Rhea said ruefully. 'I wish I could like her, Michael, but I don't.'

'I've always found her completely heartless when it comes to getting her own way,' he said, 'but Nicolas will not listen to such logic, which is a pity. He always lets her do as she likes here—always did as far back as I can remember. It had something to do with her having no one to protect her—no responsible male, I suppose I mean. He was sorry for her because her father had died while she was still a schoolgirl. She has full use of the house whenever she wants to come to the island, which isn't very often these days, I gather. She used to come a lot with Kyria Metaxas in the old days, but that seems to have cooled off a bit. Alexandra Metaxas gave her her first chance in modelling, but I think she expected Daphne to stay and work in Athens. No big deal, really, when you think in terms of the world.'

'*You* came back from New York,' Rhea pointed out. 'Was that not a big enough deal when you finally considered it?'

'It was a point of honour,' he said quite solemnly. 'I couldn't let the family down by *not* going, when they needed a Christos to hold the reins in America.'

'And now you are back for good,' she mused. 'I think I envy you very much.'

'I have an idea you'll stay at Volponé as long as you can,' he said unexpectedly. 'Don't let Daphne chase you away, Rhea, whatever you do.'

'*Kalinikta!*' everyone was calling. 'Good night! Good night!'

Nicolas came back to stand on the terrace, smiling crookedly.

'We are almost out of wine,' he announced. 'Tomorrow I must go down to the *hora* and order some more. I didn't expect a surprise party, but Daphne does these things. I can imagine that she also arranged tomorrow's lunch party on board the yacht at the shortest notice. You'll come, of course?'

Rhea faced him in the mellow lantern light.

'I haven't been invited, Nicolas,' she said as steadily as she could, 'and I wouldn't dream of going without being asked.'

'But it was understood,' he said, 'I'm quite sure of that. You're my guest.'

'I think I would rather work on the dig,' she told him firmly. 'It's the only way I'll gain experience.'

He hesitated.

'I've never heard anyone refusing an invitation to a party on a yacht before,' he said with some astonishment. 'I'm sure Philip would like to have you, and certainly Ida would. You made quite a hit with her, as a matter of fact.'

'I don't think this is entirely Ida's party, or Philip's either,' Rhea suggested. 'I think it might be strictly for Daphne's friends.'

'Rhea,' he said, 'you're being difficult and I've already promised to go. Why not accept with a good grace? I don't think Daphne meant to exclude you.'

'All the same,' she told him untruthfully, 'I'd rather go and dig!'

Early the following afternoon he returned to the excavations alone.

'I thought Daphne and her troops were going to rush up reinforcements,' Ariana remarked, tossing back her dark mane of hair as she looked up at him. 'We've just finished lunch.'

'There was plenty to eat on the yacht,' he said, 'but I decided not to stay after the first round of drinks. It's heavy going if you eat too big a lunch and set to work immediately afterwards. Besides,' he added, discarding the linen jacket he had worn to the party, 'I can't expect people to work up here while I take my ease on board a luxury yacht, can I?'

'You're the boss,' Ariana said, 'but—yes, it would look bad, I have to admit. We need your advice, Nicos, about some more pottery we've found, and Michael thinks he has uncovered an ikon. Could it be, do you think?'

The pottery proved to be very ordinary and from the same kitchen equipment as the other fragments they had found, but the ikon was quite different. They spent most of the afternoon cleaning and identifying it, wholly absorbed in their task until Nicolas finally laid it aside to be checked and dated ready for his first exhibition.

Daphne put in a tardy appearance in the late

afternoon with Philip Xilas, who expressed a great deal of genuine interest in their latest finds.

'What do you mean to do with the ikon?' he asked.

'If it's important I'll offer it to the museum in Athens,' Nicolas told him. 'If not, I can use it for my own museum here on Norbos, where it really belongs. We've got enough artefacts now to fill our first room, and I mean to display some of the mosaics from the terrace at the house to start another section when the time comes.'

As the sun drew closer to the mountain's rim he conducted Philip round the site, while Daphne sat on the warm stones of the surrounding wall, waiting for them.

'Come back to the yacht,' she invited as they gathered up their tools. 'You disappointed us when you didn't stay for lunch.'

Philip turned politely to Rhea and Ariana.

'We would like you to come also,' he said. 'Ida is so much enjoying herself here that we mean to stay for several days before we move on to Crete. It will give us great pleasure to return your hospitality.' He looked pointedly at Michael. 'You will come?' he asked. 'The more the merrier, as the saying goes!'

'We go tomorrow,' Ariana pointed out, 'and we haven't done any packing yet.'

'I suppose you will have to take them back to Piraeus,' Rhea overheard Daphne saying to Nicolas. 'Don't waste too much time—though you know that I won't run away!'

She did not hear Nicolas's reply—did not want to hear it, she assured herself angrily, but Daphne's dark brows were drawn together in a frown when she finally turned to look at her cousin.

'That's all settled, then,' Philip said. 'We'll look for you some time around eight o'clock.'

They walked down the steep road to the *hora* just after eight and out along the mole to where the big white yacht was anchored in the tiny harbour, dwarfing Nicolas' little caique into insignificance, but Rhea would rather have been going aboard the caique than

climbing sedately aboard the elegant *Swordfish* to be
greeted by Daphne at her spiteful best.

'I wonder if I should have told you not to bother to
dress,' she remarked as she passed them on to their
hostess. 'We find it much more convenient on board
just to change into another pair of trousers and a pretty
shirt. Skirts do get in the way, you know, especially
when one moves around.'

'We only have *one* skirt and one shirt with us,
apart from our working jeans and T-shirts,' Ariana
told her. 'We considered it would be all we would
need.'

They 'moved around' so easily on the *Swordfish*,
Rhea discovered, because it was so big and so luxurious
and not at all like the cramped little caique lying
placidly against the mole, but the smaller yacht had
much more character, especially when its trim white
sails were spread in the sun and its clean-cut white hull
cut through the turquoise water like the playful
dolphins which had followed it most of the way from
the mainland.

'Why the yearning look?' Nicolas asked, seeing her
standing alone at the rail. 'Don't tell me you would
rather be on board the caique.'

'How did you guess?' She turned to look at him in
the brilliant light of the moon. 'It was exactly what I
was thinking, as a matter of fact. All this——' she
included the well-lit deck behind them and the sound of
voices and the clink of glasses coming from the main
saloon '—doesn't feel like being at sea.'

'It's one way of doing it,' he said, 'if you have plenty
of money to indulge your whim, but I know what you
mean about being at sea.' He leaned both arms along
the rail, looking down at the dark ripple of water
beneath them. 'The *Swordfish* has one advantage, I
suppose. It's almost too big to be at the mercy of a
storm and we do get them in this part of the
Mediterranean. The Cyclades attract their fair share of
rough weather now and then when conditions can be
really bad. Mostly when the *meltémi* blows or we feel
the after effects of an earth tremor somewhere on the

Turkish mainland. Otherwise the Islands are a paradise for small yachts, and thank goodness, there are dozens of safe little anchorages all round the coast to scuttle into when the weather turns sour.'

'Don't disillusion me about your weather!' Rhea laughed. 'I've come prepared for perfection and I refuse to change my mind.'

'What do you think of Norbos?' he asked unexpectedly.

'I love it,' she answered spontaneously. 'I'm just beginning to realise what it means to "walk where ancient feet have trod". This afternoon when I dug up that piece of pottery it was like holding part of the past in my hand. I had to wonder about the people who had used it, about their way of life, whether they were grand or humble, and whether they had problems just like ours. It all gelled into a new experience as far as I was concerned. It was a new world I had never touched before.'

'You're going to enjoy working with us from now on,' he predicted, 'and that's the *raison d'être* for your enthusiasm.'

'I am enjoying it,' she admitted truthfully, 'but another part of it could be the memory of my father and how much of himself he gave to his absorbing hobby. It lasted him all his life,' she added thoughtfully, 'although he never came back to Greece. Perhaps he found that he couldn't return after my mother died—after he lost his love.'

They stood in silence under the night sky, watching the ripple of dark water along the hull to where the moonlight caught it at the stern.

'Is that why you came?' he asked, at last. 'To find the truth?'

'About my father?' She clasped her hands together on the rail. 'I've always known it, Nicolas. He was a man of great integrity who lived his life according to his beliefs. He would never have done anyone else an injury, but if he did he would feel a sense of guilt for a very long time.'

'And your mother?' he asked. 'But, there, you hardly

knew her, did you? She died while you were still a child.'

'He tried to make up for that,' Rhea said. 'He tried as best he could.'

Nicolas shifted his position to look at her.

'And you are his daughter,' he mused. 'What am I to make of all this?'

She looked up at him.

'I'd like it if we could be friends,' she said.

'And we are not yet friends?'

'I don't know. I can't be quite sure.' She stumbled over her explanation. 'When we were at Delphi it seemed so easy, but since then——'

'Since then?' he prompted.

'I don't know,' she repeated. 'Everything seems to have been turned on its head.'

He laughed, putting an arm about her shoulders.

'I wouldn't worry *your* head about that sort of thing,' he said. 'It's a topsy-turvy world and we can't do very much about it except to look for Hope at the bottom of Pandora's chest.'

'But think of all the nasty things that flew out when she first lifted the lid!' Rhea exclaimed. 'I think I'd rather not look than meet with such disaster and pain.'

'I don't think you would shut the lid quite so quickly, all the same,' he decided. 'Pandora was probably afraid.'

'Perhaps I'm equally afraid.' She was thinking about her first encounter with love, of the pain and disaster it had brought in its wake. 'I might even be tempted to lock the chest and run away.'

'Not you!' he said, looking down at her. 'You're made of sterner stuff.'

'You don't know me,' she protested. 'I'm a coward at heart.'

She moved away from his imprisoning arm, trying to laugh.

'I refuse to believe that.' He turned towards the lighted doorway further along the deck. 'Perhaps we'd better go below,' he suggested. 'It must be almost time to eat.'

She followed him reluctantly, aware that their moment of intimacy had gone and might never return.

For the remainder of the evening they mingled with Philip Xilas's other guests, chattering about shared experiences and further adventures in and around the magic circle of the Cyclades.

'We must teach you to water-ski,' Jason Papadam told her, 'and perhaps you would like to wind-surf in the bay where it's calm enough to learn and fall in without being hurt.'

'The only injury will be to your pride,' Philip Xilas assured her, 'but you must remember that it's a difficult sport. It takes great strength of the arms and leg muscles, I have to warn you, and very much perseverance. Nicolas will teach you, no doubt, if he thinks you're up to it,' he added confidentially in her ear.

Nicolas was handing round delicacies from the lavish buffet Ida had provided, and people were carrying them out on deck to eat in the moonlight, chasing away the privacy they had enjoyed such a short while ago. It had been no more than a moment stolen from time, Rhea thought, an echo of the ecstasy she had known at Delphi in the shadow of the Tholos when the world itself had seemed to stand still.

At midnight they walked back towards the house in a small procession, laughing when they stumbled on the steep incline through the sleeping *hora* with its square white houses casting their ink-black shadows on the pavement and the dome of the church standing out starkly on the cliff above. The stars had paled before the brightness of the moon and there was no need for the torch Ariana had brought, but she switched it on when they reached the gate in the courtyard wall.

'It's one o'clock,' she observed. 'It's really tomorrow!'

They left early the following morning because of the journey they had to make by car after they reached Piraeus, but there was still a certain amount of excitement about riding down to the bay on the mules with their luggage and finding themselves once again on board the caique.

The Xilas family came to wish them *bon voyage*, standing on the deck of *Swordfish* to wave as Michael cast off and the caique nosed her way carefully along the mole.

'We'll be here next weekend if this weather holds,' Philip Xilas assured them. 'See you then!'

And Daphne would be there with them, Rhea thought, unless she decided to return to Volponé in their wake.

Her cousin put in a tardy appearance with Jason Papadam as they set the sails and drifted away.

'Sorry, Nicos!' she called across the widening stretch of blue water. 'I slept late, as usual. See you anon!'

Nicolas waved but did not answer as he steered the caique across the bay and out between the sheltering headlands. It was goodbye to Norbos for another week.

He appeared distracted on the return journey to the mainland, although it was a quiet day bright with sunshine and a helpful breeze had sprung up to fill their sails long before they reached the rocky promontory of Sounion with the white columns of Poseidon's temple standing like a beacon above the waves.

Michael and Ariana were loath to part when they reached Piraeus.

'Will you be coming with us next weekend?' Ariana asked as they tied up at the jetty. 'Nicolas could do with your help.'

'I may have a boat of my own by then,' Michael teased her.

'Do you mean you're going to buy a yacht?' she demanded excitedly.

'Could do,' he said. 'So I would be going back to Norbos under my own steam.'

'Steam?' she objected.

'No more than a figure of speech. I suppose I should have said "sails",' he grinned. 'It will probably be a caique. I'll let you know, and I might even let you christen it if it hasn't already got a name.'

'It must be new in that case,' Ariana exclaimed, 'because it isn't lucky to change a yacht's name!'

'I don't believe in luck,' he said.

'You should. It's tempting fate not to.'

'You're a heathen!' he laughed. 'See you next weekend, if I must!'

When he had gone Nicolas brought round the Renault and they packed their grips into the back seat, waving him a reluctant goodbye.

'Do you think he will go back to the island?' Rhea asked as they drove away.

'It would be too late to start out now,' Ariana decided. 'Besides, he has to work. No, I don't think he'll go back till Friday, even though Daphne might still be there.'

When they finally reached Volponé John Karousis was waiting for them on the terrace, smoking an evening pipe in the last of the sunshine.

'How did you enjoy the trip?' he asked, putting the pipe aside. 'Did it come up to your expectations?'

'We enjoyed it very much,' Ariana told him, 'till Daphne put in an appearance with some of her wealthy friends and spoiled everything. After that nothing seemed to go as we had planned. Nicolas wanted me to do some cataloguing for him, but now I expect Daphne will do it. She is very clever, that one. It would have been something for Rhea to do also—to help me—but Nicolas did not make a final decision.'

'Which was most unusual for him,' John Karousis observed. 'He is a man of firm convictions, I would say. Is he returned to the island?'

'No. He brought us back to Piraeus and tied up the caique for the night. I don't think he will go back.'

Evadne, who had been listening at the kitchen door, hurried away, her lips firmly compressed, grim-faced and angry about something she had just heard.

It would be some time before their evening meal was ready, a time to sit in the shadows and talk. When Ariana hurried after her aunt Rhea decided to show her grandfather the torque and ask his advice about offering it to Nicolas.

'I have something to show you—something very precious to me—and I need your advice.' She paused beside the old man's chair. 'I know you will understand,' she added before she turned away.

Mounting the shallow stairs to her room, she could hear Evadne in the kitchen issuing orders, but Ariana had already disappeared. The door of her own room lay open and she showered and changed into a sleeveless cotton dress before she looked for the torque.

Quite sure that she had returned it to the top drawer of her dressing-chest, she searched the others just in case she had made a mistake in her haste to join her cousin in the car for their journey to Piraeus, but there was no sign of the necklet.

Unbelieving, she searched again, her hands unsteady now as she put her personal belongings aside to look into every corner.

'What have you lost?' Her aunt was standing suddenly in the doorway of her room.

'My necklet.' Rhea's heart had sunk at the thought of such a loss. 'It was here when I left for Norbos. I'm sure of that because I half intended to take it with me.'

'Then you must have done,' Evadne said coldly. 'Otherwise, how is it lost? We are not thieves in this house.'

Rhea apologised for the thought she never had.

'I'm sorry, Aunt Evadne. I didn't mean to accuse anybody,' she said. 'It's just that—the necklet means so much to me. It was my father's last gift—something he had kept for me over the years because he had once given it to my mother. It was a love token and I cherished it greatly.'

'Young people are often careless,' Evadne said as she turned away. 'Perhaps you should look elsewhere.'

The coldness of her tone and her obvious lack of sympathy struck bleakly across Rhea's heart, although she had already acknowledged the fact that her aunt did not like her.

That was by the way, however, and she began to search again, in her wardrobe, in the shallow drawer of her writing-table, even in the canvas grip she had taken with her to the island, panic growing as she was forced to acknowledge her irretrievable loss.

'What's happening?' Ariana asked, coming from her own room. 'Have you lost something?'

'My necklet—the torque,' Rhea explained, her eyes dark with despair. 'It was here when we left for Norbos and now it's gone. I'm sure I put it away in this drawer, but I can't find it now.'

'You certainly seem to have looked everywhere.' Ariana took in the chaos of the normally tidy room. 'Have you asked anyone if it was found?'

'I've only spoken to Aunt Evadne, and she felt that I had insulted everyone by even mentioning my loss. She thought I was accusing the entire household when I wasn't.'

'She would take it that way.' Ariana started to tidy up the room. 'Aunt Evadne rarely forgives an insult, so you must be careful what you say to her. She is not a happy woman.'

'I don't know what to do,' Rhea admitted sadly. 'I don't want to upset Grandpapa or 'Mama, either. They have been so kind to me in their separate ways. I can only tell you, Ariana, because we have so much in common.'

'And we love each other!' Ariana put her arm around her neck, emphasising her sympathy. 'I know exactly how you feel about things going wrong in this way, but now we must go downstairs and pretend for Grandpapa's sake that nothing has happened.'

'I meant to ask his advice about the necklet,' Rhea explained, 'because I thought of giving it to Nicolas for his museum, but I suppose he wouldn't have accepted it, anyway, since it was a fake.'

'A copy,' Ariana corrected her with amazing intuition. 'It could never have been a fake when it meant so much to you.'

'I told Grandpapa I had something to show him—something very precious,' Rhea said heavily. 'How can I possibly explain to him?'

'Nicolas has come,' Ariana told her belatedly. 'You may not have to explain until tomorrow.'

'Nicolas?' Rhea's heart seemed to miss a beat. 'I wonder why?'

'Oh, he had some business to discuss with Grandpapa and he walked over from Florina to talk with him. He often does this, you understand. He also brought a list and the cards we will be using when we start the cataloguing, so we will have plenty of work to do before we return to Norbos next weekend.' Ariana took her arm. 'We will not mention your lost necklet just yet,' she suggested. 'Not till we have searched again.'

Nicolas was standing at the head of the terrace steps when they went down. He looked relaxed and blissfully content, smoking a small cheroot while John Karousis puffed away at his pipe while they talked. It was a typically Greek scene of moving hospitality between an old man and his more vigorous neighbour, and although they might have been arguing heatedly about business or politics a moment ago they turned with one accord to greet Rhea and Ariana when they made their appearance at the open door of the house.

'I followed you home,' Nicolas told them, 'but I had to call in at my office on the way for some papers to sign.' He indicated a package lying on the wrought iron table where their glasses of *ouzo* had just been replenished. 'I've brought some work for you to do if you can possibly manage it,' he added.

A sudden wave of love and warmth enveloped Rhea as she sat down beside them. Nicolas had not gone back to Norbos; he was here with her grandfather, involving them still further in his plans for the future.

Inevitably he was pressed to share their evening meal. 'We must not allow you to return to an empty house,' John Karousis declared. 'You will stay with us and we will talk.'

Evadne set another place at the table, watching them as she moved to and fro between the terrace and the kitchen where she had supervised the evening meal. She hears everything, Rhea thought, without appearing to listen.

The meal they shared was excellent and much to Evadne's culinary credit. They had nibbled almonds and the pointed Kalamata olives which Nicolas appeared to like best with their *aperitifs* before moving to the table further along the terrace, where all the lamps had been lit and a great cauldron of fish broth steamed on a side table ready to be served.

When they were all seated Evadne ladled the *psarosoupa* into small bowls which Ariana passed round, first to her grandmother and then to their unexpected guest while John Karousis beamed at them all. The fish was sea bass freshly caught on the coast that afternoon, and this appeared to be his favourite. *Souvlákia* came next, the kebabs grilled to perfection on a skewer, and then everyone relaxed to consider their choice of sweet. The variety was almost overwhelming and it seemed to Rhea that her aunt had made a special effort for Nicolas's benefit because he was alone at Florina, and in need of a woman's attention.

Helping herself to a slice of Argos melon from the side table, she went back to sit between him and Ariana who was helping herself to *próveio* with a more than generous amount of honey to pour over it. Nicolas and her grandfather chose a local cheese, while Phaedra Karousis contented herself with some grapes.

It had been a most satisfying meal, for which Nicolas expressed his sincere thanks to the sombre-eyed cook.

'*Yásas*, Evadne!' he toasted her, raising his wine glass. 'You have excelled yourself tonight.'

She allowed herself a grudging smile.

'It is my work,' she reminded him. 'I have to look after the family.'

When they had returned to their chairs under the vine pergola she served their coffee from a large Turkish percolator with an air of resignation, sitting down at her father's command when the last cup was filled.

'It is time for you to rest your feet,' he said. 'You have been busy all day.'

Reluctantly almost, she sat on the terrace wall, sipping her coffee and listening to what was being said. They spoke of Norbos and Nicolas's plans for the museum on the island.

'I'd like to open it by the summer,' he decided, lighting a cheroot. 'Perhaps in June or July, and if the cataloguing could be done quickly we could plan for June with a bit of luck.'

'It's a tall order,' John Karousis remarked, 'but no doubt you will get all the help you require.'

'Ariana has already offered,' Nicolas said, 'and I have a promise from Rhea.'

'You will be overwhelmed by willing assistants when you also have Daphne,' Evadne commented sourly.

'Daphne won't stay on Norbos when she finds something to do which is more to her liking,' Ariana predicted. 'She'll go back to Rome.'

'We shall see.' Nicolas rose to go. 'Meanwhile, I have left you the cards and must hope for the best. Thank you again for helping.' He was looking down at Rhea, smiling into her eyes. 'I hope to see you at the weekend.'

They walked with him to the terrace edge to say good night—all except Evadne who stayed behind to collect the coffee cups on to a tray.

It was very late—after midnight—and no time to confuse her grandfather with the subject of her lost necklet, Rhea thought.

Saying good night to her grandparents, she preceded Ariana up the stairs.

'Tomorrow we will go to the coast,' her cousin suggested, 'to bathe in the sea, but first I will help Aunt Evadne with the housework to keep her from saying how idle we are.'

They parted at the door of Rhea's bedroom, kissing each other on the cheek.

'Don't worry about your necklet,' Ariana said. 'It will turn up, I feel sure.'

Rhea was not so sure. All evening she had been aware of a tension and her own grief at the loss of the torque, but she had tried to hide it from the two old people because they had been so pleased to welcome Nicolas in their home. On the surface it had been an occasion for happiness, but her own thoughts had been like a dark river running swiftly underneath.

She walked to her dressing-chest, pulling out the top drawer as if another search might reveal her lost necklet, turning over her underwear to stare unbelievingly at what was lying there. It was the torque.

For a moment she could not believe it. The lovely gold neck ornament shone up at her, the semi-precious stones glittering red and green and yellow in the lamplight, dearly familiar as they had always been, but she could not touch them in case all this was no more than a figment of her imagination, the wish process which would return her father's love gift to her intact.

Then, slowly and carefully, she lifted it into her hands, examining it carefully. It *was* the same. It had been here in the drawer she thought she had searched so diligently all the time.

Shaking with relief, she called Ariana to witness the miracle.

'I've found it!' she gasped when her cousin came hurrying to her door. 'In here, in the drawer I thought I had searched so carefully. Oh, Ariana, I've been such a fool suspecting everybody when it was really my own stupid fault, but I was so *sure*!'

'You were in too big a hurry,' her cousin pointed out, 'wanting to get away to Norbos and not being able to decide whether to take the torque with you or not. Aunt Evadne must have put the Evil Eye on you!'

'I don't believe in Evil Eyes,' Rhea returned sharply.

'You'd better while you live here,' Ariana said. 'Most Greeks have a strong belief in its power, especially out here in the country districts. If someone wishes you evil or is jealous of you, they can project it in your direction if they try hard enough.' She was half-laughing, half-serious. 'We also believe in the prophetic power of dreams—flowers are sorrow and honey means poison, but if you wish for great wealth you must dream about lice!'

Rhea laughed, her eyes twinkling in a mixture of incredulity and relief.

'You're making all this up!' she declared.

'No, it's true.' The small dark face was serious. 'Don't dream of flowers tonight if you don't wish your heart to be broken tomorrow!'

Alone in her room, at last, Rhea stared down at her

father's gift and in the bright lamplight it looked even more lovely than before. She would offer it to Nicolas, she decided, because she felt more strongly then ever now that it belonged on Norbos, in the museum he was so surely building to his father's memory.

CHAPTER FIVE

THERE was a telephone call for Ariana the following morning.

'It was Michael!' she announced with a radiant smile as she raced back up the stairs. 'He wants us to go to dinner with him tomorrow and he will come for us at six o'clock. He has already asked Grandpapa so there is no problem,' she rushed on. 'He says you must see Athens night life before you go back to England, and tomorrow evening is a good idea.'

Suspecting Michael's native ingenuity, Rhea was glad to accept. Of course he wanted to see Ariana again, but it was kind of him to invite them both.

'Wear your necklet,' Ariana suggested as they dressed for the occasion. 'It will look wonderful on white.'

Rhea hesitated, taking the heavy neck ornament out of the drawer where it had lain undisturbed all day.

'I don't know,' she said. 'I wouldn't like to lose it again and it really does feel heavy. I'd be weighted down with it in all this heat.'

The torque did feel overwhelmingly heavy as she held it in her hand—much, much heavier than before. Carefully she replaced it in the drawer.

'I'll wear it some other time,' she decided. 'Perhaps once before I finally offer it to Nicolas.'

Ariana had heard a car pull up on the terrace.

'It's Michael!' she cried. 'He's early, but we are almost ready.'

It was not Michael but Nicolas, and he was talking to John Karousis when they reached the terrace.

'I'm taking you to Athens,' he explained, 'to save Michael a journey. I brought my mother back to Florina this afternoon and now I'm returning to a meeting which wasn't possible this morning. Some Italians are flying in from Cairo on their way back to Rome, and they wish to kill two birds with one stone, businesswise.'

Rhea's heart was beating far too quickly for her liking as he handed her into the familiar convertible.

'Are you having dinner with us?' Ariana asked.

'Alas, no.' He looked disappointed. 'I'll pick you up later to bring you home.'

'That will be fine,' said Ariana without enthusiasm.

Her spirits rose again as they approached the capital, however.

'You're certainly going Greek,' Nicolas commented when he finally deposited them at their destination in the Pláka district. 'I hope you won't be deafened!'

'He's joking, of course.' Ariana assured Rhea as Michael came to meet them. 'Perhaps he would like to be coming also.'

'Have fun!' Nicolas said as he restarted the car and drove away.

The night was still very warm and they lingered for a moment on the steep pavement looking up at the Acropolis bathed in pale moonlight.

'Nicolas would have suggested something more fashionable, I suppose, but I thought you would like a *taverna*,' Michael said as they made their way into the small restaurant he had chosen. 'It's noisy but respectable!'

The sound of an orchestra greeted them as soon as they opened the door and because the resident soloist was singing they waited in the shadows before they were shown to their table. It was all new and exciting as far as Rhea was concerned and she allowed Michael to order for her, willing to trying anything he might recommend.

They ate at intervals, getting up to dance between courses which seemed to be the accepted fashion, or sitting quietly to listen to the sombre refrain of a folksong or the lively beat of *bouzoukia* music as it filled the room with sound.

The floor show enchanted Rhea with its colourful national costumes and traditional dances, and only the little, caged canaries hanging on the walls made her sad. Why do they do it, she wondered, when there are so many other birds around in their natural environment?

When the floor show was over she was glad of a respite as Michael claimed Ariana for another dance.

'Had enough?' Nicolas asked, slipping into the seat beside her. 'It can be heavy going.'

She turned to him in pleased surprise.

'What time is it?' she asked. 'We didn't expect you till ten.'

'It's almost that now.' He glanced at his watch. 'In Athens the night is still young. Shall we dance, or would you rather sit this one out?'

'I'd like to dance.'

He held her closely.

'I thought you might be wearing your necklet,' he said. 'I'm disappointed.'

'I'm sorry.' They were speaking lightly, yet there seemed to be an undercurrent of seriousness in his tone. 'I left it at Volponé because I thought a *taverna* dinner was hardly the right setting for it. It's only a copy, of course, but to me it's still rather special. I'll bring it to the island at the weekend,' she promised.

Wondering if she should confide in him about her suspected loss of the torque the day before, she decided against it because it all seemed rather trivial now—her anguish at its disappearance and her brush with Evadne, who had accused her of casting suspicion on the entire household when she had failed to find the necklet in her drawer.

I must have been dreaming, she thought, not concentrating properly. As she was dreaming now? Nicolas held her strongly in his arms, guiding her across the floor, and for once the *bouzoukias* had given way to the subtle magic of violins and a piano expertly played.

They danced till almost midnight when Ariana sighed and said they must go.

'It's been the most perfect evening,' she told Michael. 'I'll always remember it. *Efharistó*, Michael! *Efharistó*!'

Rhea would remember it, too, especially after Nicolas had arrived to make their number even.

The drive back to Volponé in the light of the pearl-coloured moon passed all too quickly and soon Nicolas was setting them down at their own gate.

'We'll work as hard as we can to have everything ready for the weekend,' Ariana promised. 'Rhea's printing is far better than mine, so I'm leaving her to do the cards. Thanks, darling Nicos, for bringing us home!'

She put her arm about his neck to kiss him when she got out of the car, her enthusiasm and happiness spilling over as she ran ahead across the *stoa* to the front door. Nicolas smiled, drawing Rhea gently towards him.

'*Kaliníkta!*' he murmured. 'Good night, Rhea. Sleep well and—thank you!'

He pressed his lips briefly against hers, a casual parting kiss as wholly impersonal as the one he had given her cousin, meaning as little.

During the next two days she concentrated on the work she had promised to do for him, writing industriously at the table under the vines when her permitted share of the housework was done and walking with John Karousis through the olive grove afterwards, or further afield towards the vineyards when the heat of the sun had lost its ferocity and an old man could stroll in comfort across the land he loved. Sometimes they went by mule-cart, plodding contentedly along the dusty estate roads and up on to the escarpment where Florina came into view.

'Alexandra Metaxas was always eager to buy our olive grove,' he told her once, 'but I would never sell. If it had come to their family through marriage that would have been a different thing.' He looked down at her sitting beside him. 'It may do so one day,' he reflected, 'and I will be pleased.'

Perhaps he would give it to Daphne as a wedding dowry, Rhea thought, or to Ariana. But Ariana was already very much in love with Michael, so that left only Daphne.

They set out for Norbos again at the weekend and she took the printed reference cards with her and the necklet wrapped in a silk kerchief which Ariana had given her. Nicolas met them at the yacht basin, where Michael was also waiting, more than ready to crew on the caique for a second time.

The white sails spread, they made good time along the coast and out towards the Islands, reaching Norbos in the early afternoon. Rhea found herself standing well forward as they approached the narrow entrance to the harbour, wondering if they would find it empty or still occupied by the Xilas's yacht. The mole was hidden from the open sea, sheltered behind the steep cliff of the promontory where the ruined tower looked down on the white houses of the *hora*, but in the moment when they changed course to sail in between the twin headlands she was aware of her own bitter disappointment. *Swordfish* was lying there in the sun with its full complement of guests and crew, she supposed. Daphne and Jason Papadam and Philip and Ida and Paris would all be aboard.

Paris appeared on deck as they approached.

'Hullo!' he greeted them. 'We were waiting for you.'

The others came up, smiling and waving as the caique drew alongside.

'What was it like in Athens?' Ida wanted to know. 'It's been glorious here.'

'We decided to stay,' Paris said, 'because of the dig. It really is exciting and I've been helping all week. I could go on helping,' he added tentatively, 'if you wanted me to.'

'I never turn down a genuine offer,' Nicolas assured him. 'You're recruited on the spot!'

Daphne was standing on the mole, waiting for them to moor.

'I've moved up to the house,' she said slowly. 'I knew you wouldn't mind, Nicolas. I find a small cabin terribly cramping, and the house is really more like home.'

Not even the Lodge, Rhea thought. It had to be the house, even although everyone else was at the Lodge.

Nicolas made sure of his mooring ropes before he answered her.

'I had no idea you were staying,' he said, 'but you're quite welcome so long as you haven't decided to alter everything.'

'Not really,' Daphne assured him. 'Only the sleeping arrangements.'

The mules were waiting and soon the pack animals were loaded with their luggage and the extra provisions they had brought with them.

'I'll join you later,' Daphne said. ''Bye for now!'

She was completely confident, completely in charge of the situation, Rhea thought as they rode up between the square white houses towards the pink-domed church on the headland. Daphne would never come off second best, and she had established herself at the house in their absence, whether with Nicolas's permission or not. The atmosphere would no longer be the same.

They went in through the gates in the wall to be met by Kyria Kotsovos, whose feathers appeared to be slightly ruffled.

'I did all I could to keep your room for you,' she told Ariana in passionate Greek, 'but it was of no use when Thespinis Capdistrias came. She it was who changed the rooms, putting you to the back of the house where the view is not so good.'

Ariana was clearly taken aback.

'But she knew we had that room last time,' she protested. 'It's sheer spite, if you ask me!'

'Perhaps she's trying to tell us something,' Rhea suggested, her heart sinking at the thought. 'Nicolas may have asked her to act as his hostess, and so she would have every right to change the rooms.'

'He wouldn't!' Ariana declared. 'At least, I don't think he would.'

Even Ariana was uncertain about Nicolas as she marched up the stairs with a dark frown between her brows.

The room which had been prepared for them looked towards the mountains. It had no sea view, but at least it faced east where the sun would greet them early each morning and they could see the pink dome of the church silhouetted against the deep turquoise of the afternoon sky.

It was too late to begin work at the excavations, but they walked down over the headland to see if anything else of importance had been found there in their absence. They found Daphne standing idly by as Paris

Xilas helped to wash some scraps of Byzantine pottery which had been uncovered earlier in the day.

'I'm having the Xilas' up to the house for a meal,' she told them. 'We'll dress, of course, so I hope you've brought something decent.'

'We have cotton dresses,' Ariana told her. 'Does Nicolas know about your dinner party?'

'Certainly, he knows!' Daphne declared, 'although I don't really have to ask him.'

So Daphne had taken over, even to the point where she arranged Nicolas's entertaining for him in his absence.

When they returned to the house she was busy in the kitchen supervising the meal Kyria Kotsovos was preparing.

'Let's make ourselves scarce,' Ariana suggested. 'Mama Kotsovos is about to explode!'

At eight o'clock the yacht party arrived to be greeted at the gate by Nicolas. Rhea saw them crossing the gravelled terrace in front of the house and her hand went automatically to the torque which she had clasped about her neck a few minutes ago. The love token felt heavy and constricting at her throat, but she walked slowly across the hall to meet Nicolas's guests with a welcoming smile on her lips.

Daphne chose to make an entrance a few minutes later, appearing at the head of the stairs in an inappropriate purple dinner-gown and waiting for a split second till Nicolas looked up at her. Did I dream of flowers last night, Rhea wondered, knowing herself finally in love with Nicolas.

Daphne noticed the necklet immediately, although Rhea's hand had gone to her throat involuntarily, as if to hide it.

'How beautiful!' she exclaimed, reaching her cousin's side. 'Have you shown it to Nicolas? I'm sure he will be interested, though it must be no more than a copy.'

Rhea could feel Nicolas's eyes on her, on the necklet at her throat, and a wild colour rose into her cheeks.

'I promised to bring it,' she told him, a cold sensation of loss filling her heart. 'I thought I would offer it to you for your museum.'

Daphne laughed.

'Nicolas couldn't possibly exhibit a fake,' she declared. 'Everything in the musuem must be genuine.'

Nicolas was still gazing at the torque, but Kyria Kotsovos had come to announce that their meal was ready and he led his guests into the formal dining room where the table had been laid.

Throughout the meal Rhea's hand went again and again to the necklet, feeling its weight now as never before. How heavy it was, almost bowing her head down, she thought, and the sharp little stones seemed to be cutting into her flesh! Somehow she could not offer it to Nicolas again, but on the terrace later, when his guests had gone back to the yacht and Daphne had gone to her room he stood beside her in the amazing starlight and asked if he might see it.

She turned, allowing him to unclasp the torque from her neck, his fingers warm against her flesh for a moment, but when she looked up at him at last, he was frowning.

'Rhea,' he said, 'this is no fake. It's the real thing, the missing artefact I've been searching for over a number of years.'

Stern and cold, he continued to look down at her, condemnation struggling with some other emotion in his eyes which she was unable to name.

'Your father found it originally,' he added flatly, 'but he gave it to my father and then it went missing.'

Shock swept over her like a surging tide. What was he implying? What was he trying to say? She stood before him, choked with fury and a desperate black despair.

'Are you suggesting that my father stole it?' she demanded in a strangled whisper. 'Nicolas, is that really what you believe?'

He turned from her.

'What other explanation would you offer?' he asked coldly.

'None!' She felt completely shattered. 'I almost can't believe this,' she rushed on, 'and I can't possibly stay on Norbos now. It would be impossible for us to work together after this.'

'Nothing is proved,' he said briefly. 'You are half way through the cataloguing and 'Ana needs your help.'

'But you're in charge,' she pointed out bleakly, trying to steel herself to this parting. 'Nicolas, you must see how impossible it would be for me to go on working on the dig.'

He gazed across the starlit garden beyond the terrace wall, his lips sternly compressed and all his kindness gone.

'You must please yourself,' he said, crossing the shadowy courtyard to his own domain.

Daphne made the most of their quarrel the following day, quick to see that Nicolas's attitude to Rhea had changed dramatically.

'I've decided to stay on the island,' she announced, 'and Philip thinks they may as well be in a safe harbour for a day or two longer instead of wandering aimlessly across the Aegean looking at other islands. Don't worry about the cataloguing,' she said to Nicolas, 'I'll help all I can. Really, I'm quite good at that sort of thing,' she added.

'I won't work with Daphne,' Ariana declared when she was alone with Rhea. 'I just can't!'

'You must,' Rhea told her. 'We can't both let Nicolas down.'

Nicolas was tidying up the site, leaving only one small section to be worked over for possible finds, but there was still a lot of sorting out to do. By midday, however, he called a halt and they converged on the *hora* to plan an afternoon's sport. Michael and one of the students had brought sail-planes with them and the *Swordfish* boasted a small speedboat which was pressed into service to allow them to water-ski.

'Come aboard and have something to eat with us,' Ida invited when she saw Rhea standing on the mole. 'We keep a buffet lunch going until about three o'clock.'

'I ought to go back to work, I suppose.' Rhea looked up towards the plateau. 'I'm helping Ariana with the cataloguing for Nicolas's museum.'

'He's eager to get it finished. It means quite a lot to him, I understand,' Ida said.

'Yes.' From where they stood they could see the small building where the artefacts would eventually be housed standing at the end of the village street. 'It isn't big, but I think it will be adequate, and already we have enough to fill the first room.'

Ida was immediately interested.

'Will you be here for the opening?' she asked.

'I don't know.' Rhea had already accepted the fact that she could no longer work on Norbos. 'I don't think so.'

'You've done most of the cataloguing, I hear.' Ida made room for her in the tender. 'Please come on board,' she said. 'Nobody is going to work this afternoon.'

When they reached *Swordfish* she led the way along the deck to where a generous buffet was laid out under a white awning.

'Nicolas must be very grateful to you,' she suggested, 'especially when you're supposed to be on holiday. How long do you hope to stay in Greece?'

'I—came for a month.'

'But you will stay longer because you have fallen in love with our country!' Ida suggested. 'And I understand you are also half Greek, so it must be difficult for you—the thought of going away.'

It *was* difficult. Rhea's heart contracted with pain even at the possibility, but eventual parting seemed inevitable.

Filling her plate, she carried it forward to watch the others at play. Michael was poised on a sail-plane alongside the hull and Nicolas drifted out to join him.

'Race you to the headland!' Michael challenged.

'I'll give you the necessary start!' Suddenly Nicolas was looking directly up at her. 'Would you like to try?' he asked.

Swiftly she shook her head.

'I wouldn't last five minutes,' she protested. 'I'm going for a quiet snorkel when I've finished eating.'

It wasn't easy to pretend, to act as if nothing had

happened between them, and even when she put on her swimsuit and swam with Paris and Ariana in the bay she was conscious of a tension which was difficult to hide.

Daphne disdained all water sports, lying on a sun-lounger all afternoon until it was time to return to the house as the sun set behind the mountain rim. In the evening, however, she came into her own, acting the part of hostess to Nicolas's host with consummate charm as they entertained the yacht party in their turn.

There was another whole day to put in, Rhea thought next morning, twenty-four hours in which to avoid Nicolas as best she could although every nerve in her body cried out to be with him. He was still busy at the excavations, and suddenly she knew that she had to apologise to him for all she had said in the heat of the moment when he had first seemed to doubt her father's integrity.

Walking back from the pink-domed church with Ariana she saw him gathering up his tools at the far end of the site where he had evidently been working all morning.

'I'll catch you up,' she said to her cousin. 'I—feel I should apologise to Nicolas.'

'Whatever for?' Ariana wanted to know.

'I—we had a difference of opinion. It was about the torque. He seems to think it's genuine.'

Ariana stopped in her tracks.

'Not a copy, do you mean? Well, that certainly would make a difference.'

'Yes,' Rhea admitted. 'But I'm not convinced, and I would never believe that my father stole it.'

'Is that what Nicolas thinks?'

'He didn't say so in so many words, but—yes, he must have thought so. That's why I told him I could never work with him again.'

'You *have* got a problem,' Ariana agreed. 'What did he say?'

'He was as angry as I was. He told me I must please myself about working for him, but he also pointed out that you would need help to finish the cataloguing.'

'I could hardly do it all by myself, not if it's to be finished by June,' Ariana pointed out. 'As for Daphne taking it over, she would *never* finish it. She has too much to do elsewhere. "Too many firearms in the heat", do you say?'

'"Irons in the fire",' Rhea supplied. 'That's beside the point, though. I was hurt and I lost my temper and now I feel I've let everyone down, including my father.'

'You don't believe he gave the original necklet to your mother, then?'

'No, I don't, and I'm still not sure that it *is* the original one,' Rhea declared.

'Well, go and argue it out with Nicolas again,' her cousin advised. 'He is very understanding.'

'He didn't sound it when he saw the necklet!'

'He could have been angry too, and very surprised.'

'Yes,' Rhea agreed, 'I have to think of that.'

'I'll wait for you at the house.'

'Yes—thanks, Ariana!'

Rhea turned back towards the site only to find Daphne standing there arm-in-arm with Nicolas, her light silk shirt and matching skirt blowing in the wind, her free hand holding back the tendrils of long hair from her forehead as she pointed out something of interest to her beside the wall.

I couldn't speak to him, Rhea thought; not with Daphne there. I couldn't expect him to understand.

Blinded by sudden tears, she walked across the headland, following Ariana to the house.

It wasn't easy to avoid Nicolas when they were practically living under one roof, but the evening passed eventually with a repetition of the sing-song they had enjoyed so much the evening before, and it was almost midnight again when Michael and the students returned to their own quarters at the Lodge.

'You will be going back tomorrow morning,' Daphne said hopefully as they prepared to say good night. 'Early, I suppose?'

'Yes,' Nicolas agreed. 'Can we give you a lift?'

'I'll come with you as far as Athens,' Daphne

decided. 'I really must report for work.'

They set sail the following morning, leaving *Swordfish* still lying in the bay. Philip Xilas was determined to stay for a few more days to enjoy the comparative privacy of Norbos, and he hoped that they would meet again. 'We may still be around when you return,' he called from deck to deck as they passed. 'It's a fisherman's paradise here!'

'Make the most of it,' Nicolas called back. 'And thanks for the use of the speedboat.'

The journey to Piraeus was uneventful. Rhea sat on deck most of the way while Daphne sunned herself in the cockpit where she could talk to Nicolas at the wheel. If he was still angry and disillusioned about the necklet he refused to show it, but the line of his mouth seemed sterner and his jaw tighter as they drew nearer their destination. He won't ask me to come again even if I offer, Rhea thought bleakly. Nothing that has happened between us will alter his opinion now.

Back at Volponé she packed up the torque and sent it to him at Florina, so short a distance across the olive grove which was more like a barrier now.

'It is yours by right,' she wrote in the letter which accompanied it. 'I can't keep it now.'

The following evening he returned it personally. They were sitting out on the *stoa* in the last of the sunshine when he walked towards them, the little package which she recognised immediately in his hand.

'I'd like to speak to you, Rhea,' he said. 'Have you a moment?'

Evadne was there, and Ariana and her grandfather.

'I—sent you a message.' Rhea got to her feet almost reluctantly. 'About the necklet,' she added.

'That's what I want to talk to you about,' he said.

John Karousis laid down his pipe.

'It's cold,' he complained, 'I'm going in. There's more sun on the other side of the house.'

Ariana followed him, but Evadne stood her ground.

'You will take something to drink, Nicolas?' she asked. 'And perhaps you will stay for dinner with us.'

'I'd like to very much,' he said, 'but my mother is at

Florina with a batch of accounts she wants me to look at, and I have been away all weekend.'

'Then you must not stay,' Evadne agreed, still reluctant to leave them alone.

'Another time,' he suggested, 'in the circumstances.'

When her aunt had gone Rhea stood looking out over the gravelled terrace where the shadows were gathering until Nicolas put the necklet down on the table between them.

'I've come to apologise,' he told her without preliminary. 'A lot was said in the heat of the moment, Rhea, and I had no right to doubt you without absolute proof.'

'But—you still think the torque is genuine?' The words choked in her throat. 'It leaves a doubt, doesn't it? The sort of doubt that will grow and grow every time we think about it because, you see, I'm still convinced that it's just a clever copy of the original, as my father said. I've got to think that, Nicolas,' she pleaded. 'I've *got* to believe in him. Surely you can understand?'

He took the necklet from its wrapping, holding it out to her.

'Wear it,' he said. 'Your father gave it to you.'

'I couldn't!' She stood back, looking down at her father's love-gift. 'Not until I know for certain.'

'What difference will it make? I'm giving it back to you.'

She recoiled before the certainty in his tone.

'Then—you *do* think it was stolen!' she cried. 'You've convinced yourself that it's the genuine torque and—and he took it because he thought it belonged to him—because he found it!' She tried to stifle the emotions that were choking her. 'He would never have betrayed your father in such a way.'

'Rhea,' he said, 'we simply don't know. It happened many years ago and there were other passions involved. We have no right to judge either of them. An old love affair, an old rivalry, long since forgotten. What have we to do with it, after all?'

'It was your father and mine, both in love with the same woman!'

'You told me your parents were happy together.' He took her by the shoulders, turning her to face him. 'That makes a difference, I think, and the torque means nothing in comparison. Perhaps you don't agree,' he added when she could not answer him, 'but it's certainly how I feel and how my mother would feel if she knew. Contrary to speculation, she did not regret her marriage, even if it might have been on the rebound as far as my father was concerned. They were good companions, Rhea, for many years.'

She looked back at him unhappily.

'What are we going to do?' she asked.

'Forget all about the necklet,' he said, 'and go on working at the dig.'

That was all. He walked away into the shadows, tall and straight as she would always remember him, crossing the gravel and going down by the terrace steps towards the olive grove, where he was finally lost to sight.

The following afternoon she took the torque to the Athens Museum, where she left it to be assessed by an expert.

She had made the journey by bus, explaining to Ariana that she had to be alone, and for once her cousin refrained from questioning her motives, saying that she would get on with the cataloguing in her absence.

'Unless you would wish me to come for you and bring you back again?' she had added helpfully.

'I'll do some shopping,' Rhea had suggested, 'and I've got a bus timetable. I'll be back before you can miss me!'

Walking along Patission Avenue she was aware of a vague relief, although there had been doubt in her heart when she had first decided to take the necklet to be assessed. It was as if she distrusted Nicolas or at least his judgment, and she had not wanted to do that.

Hesitating on the corner of Sophocleus, she bought stamps at the Post Office and was coming away when she saw Nicolas getting out of one of the light grey taxicabs which seemed to be everywhere. Subconsciously she drew back, but he had already seen her.

'Rhea,' he said, 'this is amazing! Of all the people to meet in Athens when I was least expecting you! Are you on a cultural trip, or just going on a shopping spree with Ariana?'

'I'm not with Ariana,' she said, her heart beating twice as fast as normal. 'I'm on my own.'

His eyebrows shot up as he looked across the busy road to where a seething mass of Athenians were fighting to board a yellow trolley-bus.

'It's the rush hour,' he explained. 'Have you eaten?'

She shook her head.

'Not yet.' She drew a deep breath. 'Nicolas, I've been to the Archaeological Museum.'

'Then you must certainly be in need of some light refreshment!' he decided. 'Come to lunch with me.'

He took her arm, but she did not move forward with him.

'I went there with the torque,' she said.

He looked down at her and for a moment she thought there was anger in his eyes.

'You need not have doubted my word,' he said briefly. 'I'm well acquainted with the copyist's art. My mother has fakes offered to her almost every day.'

'I had to do it.' She stood looking up at him in the bright spring sunshine, her eyes full of pain. 'It concerned my father's integrity. If—what you believe is true some part of me will be destroyed, and I will never be able to trust anyone again.'

He led her purposefully across the busy thoroughfare, signalling for an empty taxi when they reached the other side.

'I see your point of view,' he allowed brusquely, but she knew that he was still unwavering in his opinion that her necklet was the original torque.

'But you will never be able to forgive me—or my father—if I'm proved wrong.'

'It isn't a question of forgiveness.' He opened the taxi door. 'It has something to do with trust.'

She hesitated on the pavement.

'Yes, I see that,' she acknowledged beneath her breath.

He put a hand under her elbow.

'Get in,' he said, 'and we will forget about the torque for a couple of hours. I'm picking up my mother to take her to lunch. It is rarely we have time to meet each other in the middle of the day, and this is her birthday.'

'Oh!' She was already in the car and he was giving his instructions to the driver. 'Nicolas,' she protested, 'you must put me down somewhere. I can't possibly come with you.'

'Why not, may I ask?'

'Because this is a special occasion—a family occasion—and your mother would have every right to object.'

When he looked round at her his eyes were full of laughter.

'You don't know my mother,' he said. 'She is the most gregarious of women, and she has already met you.'

'At Florina,' Rhea remembered. 'But that was different.' She slid to the edge of the leather seat. 'Nicolas, you must let me go.'

'You must give me a better reason than just natural shyness,' he decided, 'and I'm quite sure you are hungry. We haven't far to go.'

She sank back against the warm cushioning. 'This is all wrong,' she said. 'Your mother must want you to herself on such a special day and she wouldn't expect you to bring along a stranger.'

'I have an ulterior motive.'

She looked at him in surprise.

'What could that be?'

'I have forgotten her present.' He looked like a small boy who had committed a grave misdemeanour. 'It's unforgivable, so you must help me to choose something suitable.'

'I have no idea what she would like,' Rhea protested. 'Nicolas, this is ridiculous!'

'Not the way I see it,' he said, signalling to the driver to stop the cab. 'You're a woman and you must know better than I do—in this case,' he added a trifle drily.

They got down at the corner of a square facing the Acropolis, where an old mosque shone white in the sun.

'It's now a folk museum,' Nicolas told her before they turned into a narrow street dominated by shoe-shops. 'This is Pandróssou, but it is generally known as Shoe Lane.'

The picturesque street also seemed to support a great number of antique shops selling Greco-Roman anti-quities and Byzantine antiques and a number of other objects from a later date, together with second-hand goods from the recent past. There were coins and pottery and votive offerings of every kind—ikons and colourful pictures of saints painted on wood, and beautiful crosses encrusted with semi-precious stones which made Rhea think of the torque.

I shouldn't be here, she thought, loving every minute of it as I walk beside Nicolas, but it's something I will never forget as long as I live.

They plunged down side streets and narrow passages until they came to a small boutique on a corner with silk curtains drawn across the window and a grille at the door. Nicolas had taken her arm to guide her along the crowded pavement and he kept a tight hold on her as they approached the shop.

'In here,' he said. 'It won't take more than a minute.'

The boutique was a veritable Aladdin's cave of expensive jewellery, embroidery and opulent furs, and the proprietress approached them with a familiar air, speaking rapidly in Greek to Nicolas until he introduced his companion.

'Ah! So you have an English lady with you today,' she beamed, changing with consummate ease to Rhea's own language. 'That is very good! You wish me to show you something Miss Langford can take back to London with her to remind her of Greece?'

'Elizabeth,' Nicolas admitted, 'I am first of all looking for a present for my mother's birthday. I should have come to you a week ago.'

'You should indeed!' she reprimanded, looking around for what might be a suitable gift. 'You give me no time to select the right article.'

'I have never known you at a loss!'

'Ah!' she exclaimed after a moment. 'There is this. It will suit your mother admirably and if she should not like it—as I think she will—she must return it promptly and make her own choice.'

She held up a magnificent embroidered housecoat, placing it against her own ample bosom to show the light and shade on the carefully-stitched design.

'It is her size,' she assured Nicolas. 'She will be most pleased with it, I feel sure.'

'What do you think?' Nicolas turned to Rhea for assurance. 'Like most men I'm not too good about making a decision about ladies' clothes.'

'I would choose it for your mother,' Rhea told him without hesitation. 'She will look magnificent in it.'

'Kyria Metaxas has a wonderful taste in clothes,' Elizabeth murmured. 'She dresses entirely to suit herself.'

Nicolas took out his cheque book.

'I'm eternally grateful,' he said. 'I'm not at all good at this sort of thing, but I know she has all the jewellery she needs.'

'And Miss Langford?' Elizabeth came back with the housecoat in a black-and-gold carrier. 'Is there something you would wish to see?'

'Oh, no! Thank you very much.' Rhea backed towards the door. 'I—I'm not shopping today.'

Elizabeth was evidently too dignified to press the point.

'Another time, perhaps?' she suggested quietly. '*Efharistó!* Come again!'

Nicolas passed the carrier to Rhea as the door closed behind them.

'It will look better if you carry this,' he said. They walked back towards Pandróssou where he stopped at a small antique shop with a few articles in the window and a stencilled sign over the door in Greek. 'Come inside,' he invited when Rhea seemed to hesitate. 'She's sure to be ready.'

Alexandra Metaxas recognised her immediately.

'How nice!' she said. 'Nicolas has brought you to share my birthday!'

'I—we met at the Post Office by accident,' Rhea said. 'It wasn't planned and I don't really think I should be here intruding in your special day.'

'But you are not intruding,' Alexandra told her as Nicolas helped her into her cape. 'You are making it even more pleasurable for me. Nicolas and I would only have discussed business if we had been left alone.'

Rhea offered the black-and-gold carrier.

'He brought you this.'

With almost child-like eagerness Alexandra Metaxas opened her birthday present, shaking out the beautifully embroidered housecoat.

'But it is magnificent!' she cried. 'Nicos! You did not choose this alone!'

'Rhea helped,' he admitted. 'And Madam Elizabeth.'

'I shall want to wear it immediately!'

'We are going out to lunch.'

'Ah, yes! That is also good. I will find my handbag,' Alexandra said.

Rhea and Nicolas exchanged glances.

'She's genuinely pleased,' Rhea smiled. 'She has so much enthusiasm.'

'Sometimes too much,' he declared, 'and she takes likes and dislikes to a great many things, to say nothing about people, but I would not have her otherwise.'

'Of course not! You must be very proud of her.'

'I am. She is, of course, fiercely independent, and I have a notion that her particular line in antiques makes her a fortune.' He laughed spontaneously. 'That, by the way, has not to be mentioned!'

'What are you saying?' his mother demanded, coming through from the back premises where she had gone to collect her handbag and leave her expected gift. 'Are you telling Rhea how difficult I am to live with when I come to Florina occasionally?'

'I wish you would come more often.' He kissed her on both cheeks. 'Now, can we go? Rhea has a rendezvous at the museum at three o'clock.'

'Indeed?' Alexandra was immediately interested. 'Is someone showing you round?'

'No—it isn't quite like that——'

'Rhea wants to have something assessed.' Nicolas was holding open the door. 'It isn't important, but we have to get back by three o'clock. Have you got your keys?'

He had dismissed the explanation Rhea had been about to give, shielding her from possible embarrassment perhaps, or not wanting his mother to remember the missing artefact which they had previously sought in vain.

When he had hailed another taxi-cab he sat facing them as they were driven through the sun-drenched city streets where the tall apartments stretched like accusing fingers towards the sky.

'They point to Olympus, blaming the gods for all the architectural horrors made in the name of progress,' Alexandra observed. 'The pick-axe and the cement-mixer have done their work in my lovely Athens, making it into a modern capital city which could be anywhere in the world if it wasn't for our surrounding mountains. Do you like it, Rhea, and will you stay here?'

It was the universal question, not at all impertinent but asked out of a very real interest.

'It's something I have thought about,' Rhea admitted.

'Your grandfather would want it, for one,' Alexandra said. 'And your grandmother, although she finds it difficult to express herself in your language, I expect.'

The taxi had stopped before a grand hotel and Nicolas helped them out. Going up the marble steps to the revolving doors Alexandra added,

'You are not in the least like your cousin Daphne. More like Ariana, in a way.'

'I've grown very fond of Ariana,' Rhea smiled. 'We wrote to each other, off and on, while she was at school.'

'Which accounts for her good English. Do you think

she will marry this boy, Michael Christos, as Nicolas predicts?'

Again the forthright question, showing her interest in all that went on around her.

'He seems just right for her,' Rhea said, 'although she is still very young.'

'Eighteen is not at all too young,' Alexandra declared, 'provided she knows her own mind. Have you ever thought of getting married?'

The colour rushed into Rhea's cheeks, but she knew that only the truth would be expected.

'Once,' she admitted, 'but it didn't work out.'

'I'm sorry, but you may have gained in wisdom from your disappointment.'

'I think I have.'

They were being shown to their reserved table in the restaurant.

'I can't help feeling that I'm here under false pretences,' Rhea said when a waiter came hurrying with an extra place setting, 'but——'

'Nicolas probably swept you off your feet,' Alexandra suggested. 'He has that way with him when he is determined.'

'You're giving Rhea a bad impression of me,' Nicolas accused her with a smile. 'She will not speak to me again!'

It was such an intimate meal as they ate leisurely and discussed everything but the torque, and it was quite evident where Nicolas got his charm, although Alexandra was in no way masculine. She was tall and beautifully proportioned, like a mature Helen of Troy, and she was equally fascinating.

'Nicos!' she sighed when the meal was over and they were drinking coffee in the open courtyard, 'that was perfect and very, very kind of you. You know how much I appreciate it, especially as you are so busy a person nowadays. My present was lovely, too.' She turned to Rhea to show her pleasure. 'Thank you for helping to choose it. You must see me wearing it one of these days.'

Going down the steps into the sunshine again, Rhea thought that two hours had never passed so quickly.

'I must get to the museum.' She looked down the busy thoroughfare for the necessary taxi-cab. 'I've cut it rather fine.'

'Nicolas will take you,' Alexandra said. 'I have some shopping to do before I open the shop again at three o'clock. You can drop me off at Venízelos Avenue,' she added. 'I have an appointment at Zolatas to buy a ring.'

When they were alone again Rhea sat bolt upright on the taxi seat, experiencing all the old inhibitions about mentioning the necklet.

'I have a dreadful feeling of guilt about going to the museum,' she confessed at last, 'especially when you've given me your advice, and now—you're being so kind.'

He laughed.

'I was born kind,' he said lightly, seeing her obvious distress. 'Don't give it a second thought.'

'I—*have* to think about it,' she said earnestly. 'It is important to me.'

He allowed the taxi to travel a little further before he answered.

'I know how important it is, Rhea,' he assured her. 'Do you want me to wait for you?'

The taxi was slowing at the kerb.

'No.' More than anything else she wanted to be alone. 'This is something I must do for myself.'

She got out of the taxi, walking slowly towards the museum as he watched. It was after three o'clock, but she almost dragged her feet going along the seemingly endless stone corridor to the door at its far end to which she had been directed.

The man sitting behind the highly-polished desk nodded towards the necklet which lay before him.

'You have a very interesting piece here, Miss Langford,' he told her. 'Not valuable, you understand, but interesting. Do you wish to sell it?'

'Sell it?' She stared at him, uncomprehending for a moment. 'It—isn't mine to sell.'

'I have put a date on it for your convenience.' He picked up the torque. 'Yes—interesting,' he repeated, 'but not valuable. We have many of the same type here in the museum of equal antiquity. This, however, may mean something to you personally.'

'Yes. Yes, it does. It was found on an island—on Norbos—and I think it belongs there.'

'That is so,' he agreed, handing over her father's love-token. 'It is what you must do with it. Take it back there.'

But she would never go to the island again, she thought as she retraced her steps along the corridor where all her hopes seemed to have been shattered in less than quarter of an hour.

When she finally reached Volponé she felt as if she had been away for a lifetime. It was almost dark and Ariana had walked down to the village square to meet the bus.

'Had you a good day?' she asked. 'You look very tired.'

'I met Nicolas,' Rhea said automatically. 'It was quite by accident as I was coming out of the Post Office. He invited me to lunch. It was his mother's birthday. I thought I shouldn't intrude, but he insisted, and Kyria Metaxas was very nice about it. All the same, she must have thought it odd—a great coincidence that we should meet by chance.'

She was speaking like someone in a dream, finding the right words instinctively as they walked up the hill to the farm.

'I went to the museum—I took the torque. It was something I had to do, Ariana. They told me it was genuine.'

'Genuine?' her cousin repeated, halting on the narrow road. 'But how could that be? You have always thought it was a copy of the necklet your father discovered on Norbos.'

'That is why I had to go to the museum for advice. I had to be sure, but now I know that Nicolas was right. Ariana, you can understand what this means.' Her eyes were suddenly dark with pain. 'He can no longer trust me.'

'He can't *blame* you,' Ariana said. 'It was something you had to do.'

'It will keep me from going to Norbos again,' Rhea said. 'How can I return when this has happened?'

'He needs your help.'

Rhea smiled wanly.

'I'll go on writing the cards,' she decided, 'but I'll do it here.'

'Have you told Nicolas about this—about the torque being genuine?'

'He knew all along.'

'And it has made no difference?'

'How could it be the same? He wouldn't trust me to work on the dig now in case something else of value disappeared.'

For once Ariana was silent. They had come to the house and the familiar old building loomed up before them, warm and white and welcoming. I must give this up, too, Rhea thought, all the love and caring I wanted from the very beginning.

John Karousis was waiting for them on the *stoa*.

'You have had a good day?' he suggested, his wrinkled face creased in a broad smile. 'How did you find your way in all that dreadful traffic? Athens was never built for the motor car!'

Rhea told him what she had done, the rush of words pouring out like a river which had been dammed up too long, and he listened patiently as Ariana hurried away. When her final confession had been made Rhea took the necklet from her handbag, placing it on the table between them.

'I must return it to Norbos,' she said.

He sat looking at it for a moment, scratching his head.

'I can't understand it,' he said, at last, 'because your father spoke to me about this thing a long time ago—about getting a good copy made locally to take back to England for your mother—my lost Maria.'

'I'll never believe that he stole it,' Rhea said quickly. 'I can't.'

'You loved him greatly,' her grandfather said. 'I see how it is for you.'

Torn by the sudden fear that her father's affection for

her mother might have led him to take the original necklet as his love-gift to her, Rhea asked the wise old man what she had to do now.

'Already you have the solution in your heart,' he said gently. 'Give it back to the island. Make it your personal contribution to the museum when it is opened. You can do nothing else, no matter what it might cost you,' he added.

It had already cost her much, Rhea thought. Nicolas's friendship, and certainly his trust, and he might not accept her gift in the end. He had scorned it once before, so how could she approach him again?

Picking up the necklet, she dropped it into her handbag to carry it up to her room.

'I must go and change,' she said into the shadows where he sat beside the open door. 'Thank you, Grandpapa.'

Evadne crossed the hall ahead of her, appearing out of nowhere, it seemed. Had she been listening to what had been said on the *stoa*? It did not seem to matter.

CHAPTER SIX

THERE was still plenty of work to do on the cataloguing and the printing of the little cards which would go with each exhibit, and Rhea worked some part of each day with Ariana to make sure that nothing was overlooked. The days passed without any contact with Nicolas, and the following weekend nobody seemed to be going to the dig on Norbos.

'The site is now complete in almost every detail,' Michael told them when they met in Athens one afternoon. 'Now we have to wait for Nicolas to make his final decision about the opening of the museum. It can't be long delayed if it's to attract the summer visitors to the island,' he mused, 'and Nicolas wants to do that to safeguard the prosperity of the *hora*.'

The little township at the harbour depended entirely on the fishing industry, and if Nicolas wished to expand the island's economy a thriving tourist trade was essential. The crops they grew were enough for the islanders' immediate need, but the museum and the new excavations would bring in the visitors and add to the *hora*'s prosperity.

Another week passed without any contact between Volponé and Florina. It was early June and their lists were almost complete, but still they were not sure of a date for the opening of the museum. Then, one afternoon when they were swimming in the deserted pool at Florina, they were confronted by Kyria Metaxas at her most charming.

'I had hoped to visit you at Volponé,' she said, coming down the marble steps from the terrace to stand at the edge of the pool, 'but time is my greatest enemy! Rhea, we have not met since my birthday and that is almost three weeks ago. It is too bad of Nicolas not to have arranged something, but I believe he has been in Rome for several days.'

'Rome?' Rhea found herself repeating foolishly. 'I—had no idea.'

'He had business to attend to there and also in Switzerland—in Berne, I think. He should delegate some of his journeys, I have told him, but my advice is not always taken.'

Rhea pulled herself out of the water to find her towelling coat.

'We have used all the cards he left us,' she said, wondering if Nicolas might have gone to Rome with Daphne. 'We thought he would have sent some more. I think we need about a dozen to finish the lists.'

'Oh, yes, there was something about cards, I remember!' Alexandra pushed both hands into the pockets of the housecoat she was wearing. 'He left them in his desk before he went away. Come up to the house and I will find them for you.'

Ariana splashed out of the pool to join them.

'Is there a date set for the opening of the new museum?' she asked. 'It is now June and Nicolas said that would be an ideal time because of the tourists.'

'That was what I was coming to Volponé to see you about,' Alexandra told them as they walked up the steps. 'We have set the date for the twentieth of this month, when we hope all will be in order. It never is, of course,' she laughed, 'but if there are any defects we can cover them up for the time being. I was coming to Volponé to let you know, but I got myself very involved with the publicity in Athens. Which is really no excuse,' she allowed as they reached the house itself. 'What I was determined to do was to make sure that everyone turned up for Nicolas's great day—your grandmother and grandfather and Evadne, and you, too, Rhea. Daphne was not sure if you would still be here.'

It was the first time she had mentioned Daphne taking part in their discussions, but the knowledge that her cousin had been involved in Nicolas's preparations for his 'great day' sent a chill into Rhea's heart.

'Of course Rhea will still be at Volponé,' Ariana rushed in to say. 'I don't know where Daphne got the idea that she would be somewhere else.'

'I'm glad,' Alexandra smiled. 'Nicolas will need all the support we can give him.'

Tea was brought and afterwards Alexandra went in search of the extra cards.

'We won't need them all,' Ariana decided when she returned with the small package in her hand. 'One or two will do, and we can keep the rest for an emergency.'

On the way back to Volponé, having thoroughly enjoyed Alexandra's honey-cakes and lemon tea, she said thoughtfully,

'I'm glad she made a point of inviting *everybody*. Otherwise I think Aunt Evadne would have refused to come.'

'She might still refuse,' Rhea pointed out, 'even if Daphne will be playing a leading part. It seems likely, don't you think?'

Ariana considered the matter.

'You mean—opening the exhibition for Nicolas?'

'Yes. It's the sort of thing I could imagine her doing very gracefully.'

'She hasn't exactly done a lot to help with the actual excavations,' Ariana pointed out, 'and she doesn't know the first thing about archaeology, but perhaps that doesn't matter. She's very decorative and that may be what Nicolas wants.'

'Actresses and people like that are a great draw,' Rhea said.

'Daphne isn't an actress,' Ariana objected. 'At least, not as you would notice! She's only a model. Rhea,' she added after a moment, 'the torque ought to be there for the opening if you mean to let Nicolas have it for the museum.'

'It was my intention,' Rhea admitted, 'but I haven't seen him for almost three weeks to offer it to him.'

'You could take it to Norbos when we all go over,' her cousin suggested. 'You could print a card and we could slip it in with the other exhibits before the actual ceremony takes place. You don't actually have to *ask* Nicolas, do you?'

They made their way through the silent olive grove with her cousin's final question unanswered. Probably

she didn't need Nicolas's permission to include the
necklet, but would he refuse to take it if she asked? Or
was it just a matter of indifference to him, one way or
another? Rhea could not think so because he had said
once that he had searched for the original torque for
years. It was the measure of his interest; it was
something he had wanted for a very long time, the star
exhibit of his whole collection.

Daphne had arrived at Volponé when they finally
reached the farm. She was standing beside her mother
with a good deal of luggage surrounding them, which
suggested that someone had brought her right to the
door. Could it have been Nicolas, Rhea wondered,
although Alexandra had not expected him at Florina?

'Hullo!' their cousin greeted them. 'Had a nice day?'

She was in the best of spirits, her eyes sparkling
triumphantly and a high colour suffusing her cheeks.

'You've been swimming,' she observed. 'It's the right
sort of day for it.'

Full of confidence, she directed the disposal of her
many cases, ordering the ever-willing Yianni to carry
them upstairs to her room.

'I expect you've heard all about Nicolas's plans for
next week,' she remarked, sinking down into one of the
sun-loungers. 'He brought me home half an hour ago,
but he wouldn't stay. He's so busy. Did you see his
mother when you were at Florina? She has been doing
most of the advertising while we've been away.'

She had emphasised the 'we', utterly confident in her
newly-acquired power.

'Kyria Metaxas has invited us all,' Ariana informed
her. 'The whole family, that is.'

Daphne allowed herself a brief glance in Rhea's
direction.

'Will you go?' she asked.

'Of course!' Rhea forced the words out with an effort.
'I may even have an interest.'

'Because your father once worked on the excavations
with Kyrie Metaxas,' Daphne mused. 'But that was a
very long time ago.'

'We're dealing in time, don't you think?' Rhea asked.

'Hundreds and hundreds of years. I think that's what the exhibition is all about. No one person can really claim responsibility.'

Daphne poured herself a cooling drink.

'I'll probably be playing hostess for Nicolas next weekend,' she informed them carefully, 'when the museum is officially opened. It will help Alexandra—lessen the strain and that sort of thing. Nicolas and I have always been close.'

Perhaps, Rhea thought, she might even perform the opening ceremony as Nicolas's future wife.

The thought persisted well into the following week, haunting her dreams as Daphne spent more and more time at Florina, helping Alexandra, no doubt.

Everyone at Volponé took it for granted that Rhea would go to the island for the opening ceremony because of her father's close connection with the original dig, and she could not disappoint them when her grandparents had showered her with love and affection ever since she had arrived. Only her grandfather and Ariana knew the truth about the necklet, she thought.

They crossed to Norbos on a magnificent day of bright sunshine and blue skies, with Mount Athos shimmering in a heat haze and all the islands scattered like gems on the turquoise sea. Michael had come for them in Nicolas's caïque and even Grandmama was there in her best black with a veil tied underneath her chin to keep her hat in place. Daphne had left Volponé the day before and was already on the island when they arrived, dressed adequately in white linen with a white straw hat tilted forward over her eyes, and she wore gloves.

'Do you think she *is* going to open the museum?' Ariana whispered as they filed ashore.

'It looks like it.'

There was no sign of Nicolas. Rhea looked up towards the house but could not see any sign of life on the twisting road which led down to the *hora*. The little town itself was full of people who had come, as they had done, by sea, and dozens of strange craft were moored thickly along the mole. Rhea picked out *Swordfish* without difficulty.

'I thought the Xilas family would be here,' Ariana said, 'and I suppose Paris and Jason Papadam will be with them.'

'If you ask me, half of Athens is here!' Michael declared. 'It's a marvellous turnout. Nicolas should be very pleased.'

There was still no sign of Nicolas, but he could very well be already in the museum.

'There's a plaque of some kind,' Michael informed them. 'Someone important will unveil it, I guess, but for the moment Nicolas isn't saying who it will be.'

'He may have another announcement to make,' Rhea said.

Daphne came to stand beside them, gracious in her role of hostess, official or unofficial as the case may be. You're doubting her authority because you won't face up to the facts, Rhea told herself harshly, and you won't be able to stay at Volponé if Nicolas marries your cousin Daphne.

'I have to see Nicolas,' she said, clasping the torque closely in her hands. 'I have to give him this.'

Daphne drew back at sight of the necklet.

'Why distress him needlessly?' she demanded. 'He has already dismissed the torque from his thoughts, just as he has dismissed you! He does not need your pretty bauble to complete his exhibits, even if it is the genuine article,' she added crushingly.

Rhea stepped back, realising in that moment that her cousin had always known about the torque and might even have been the person to alert Nicolas in the first place.

She was determined, however, to put it in its rightful position among the other exhibits, taking the little card she had printed with its estimated date of origin from her handbag as Daphne moved away to mingle with Nicolas's more important guests.

'We'll go over to the museum now,' Ariana suggested. 'Have you got the card?'

Rhea nodded, feeling uncertain even now that what

they were about to do would be the right thing in the circumstances. 'The door may be locked,' she suggested nervously.

'We can go in by the side entrance. Come on!' said Ariana. 'We haven't got much time left.'

They moved swiftly along the cobbled street, climbing the flight of shallow steps to the higher level where the porticoed museum stood half in shade, half in sunlight as if guarding at least half its secret from the busy outside world.

'Everybody will be flocking up here in a minute or two,' Ariana panted. 'We *do* need to hurry.'

Following in her breathless wake, Rhea could feel the necklet cold in her hand. Supposing it was all against Nicolas's wishes; supposing he had decided not to exhibit the necklet at all?

It was too late now, she thought as they gained the higher level and the shadows lurking around the side door which could, after all, be locked. It gave to Ariana's touch, however, almost welcoming them in.

'We must be quiet,' Ariana whispered. 'We don't want to be discovered.'

'Ariana, do you think——'

'There isn't time to think! It is ten minutes to three o'clock and the main door will soon be opened. Michael says that Nicolas has had a golden key made, and I suppose he will present it to Daphne if she is the chosen one to perform the ceremony.'

'Yes,' Rhea agreed in a choked whisper, 'it's generally the custom.'

The door creaked as they pushed it wider, but they were unobserved. All was still and quiet inside, with shafts of dusty sunlight slanting in through the high, arched windows near the roof. It made a golden splendour of the floor mosaics and glistened on the brass corners of the showcases which had yet to be filled. The first two rooms were empty, waiting for future finds on the dig, and they went swiftly towards the main entrance hall where the work had been completed only the evening before. The filled show-cases stood in two ranks on either side of a powerful

bronze of Poseidon poised to hurl his trident at the
world, and on the wall behind him facing the main door
a plaque waited to be unveiled behind two short purple
velvet curtains linked by a heavy cord.

In a few minutes, Rhea thought, Daphne would pull
that cord, revealing to the world that she was Nicolas's
intended bride.

Ariana's swiftly indrawn breath was like the echo of
the sigh in her own heart, and then she saw Nicolas
standing there quite still before the veiled plaque. Half-
hidden behind one of the columns which supported the
roof, they had failed to see him until they turned the
corner, and he appeared to be entirely unconscious of
their presence for a moment as he gazed straight ahead
as if he saw in front of him the procession of the years
which had brought them inevitably to this moment of
revelation. Rhea saw his face in profile etched like one
of his country's ancient gods against the backdrop of
the marble column, and her heart seemed to miss a
beat. He was Apollo and all-powerful Heracles, the
greatest of the heroes, and Theseus, heartless seducer of
the lovely Ariadne who had almost died for love of him.
His dark brows, drawn in a frown, mirrored the
thoughts which seemed to be consuming him, and then
he turned and saw her standing there with the torque in
her hand.

'I brought this,' she said unsteadily. 'It ought to be
here, Nicolas.'

He hesitated for only a moment before he took it
from her, their fingers touching for an instant to send a
wild desire coursing through her veins as he led the way
to the showcase nearest the door which would soon be
opened triumphantly by her cousin Daphne.

'We'll put it here, where it will be seen right away,' he
said. 'After all, it's our most precious find, so far.' He
bent to unlock the case. 'Have you the necessary card?'

'It's here.' Ariana handed it over. 'It will look so
good, Nicos, in the place of honour.'

He nodded as she placed the small oblong of
cardboard beside the torque.

'Rhea printed it, like all the others,' she said.

He turned to Rhea, hesitating as he glanced at his watch.

'I have to thank you for all your hard work,' he said almost stiltedly, 'but now I must go. It is almost three o'clock and everybody will be waiting.'

They walked back through the two empty rooms to the side door, where they were met by a flood of sunlight and the murmur of the crowd gathered on the cobbles to watch the opening ceremony. The small *hora* seemed to be bulging at the seams with visitors, people whom Rhea already knew and others who were complete strangers to her, and they were all in a happy, relaxed mood as befitted the occasion. The old men of the *hora* sat on the surrounding walls running their amber worry-beads through their fingers while their wives stood sedately in the background, some of them in native costume, others simply in their Sunday clothes with their best kerchiefs over their hair and a look of shy expectation in their dark eyes. Little girls in checked dresses and white pinafores with matching mob-caps perched on their dark curls watched solemnly from the shelter of *mama*'s voluminous skirt, and boys who had earlier been mending nets along the mole had come running to share in the excitement. Two *papas* in long coats and tall black hats stood waiting beside the steps, one old and smiling behind a snow-white beard, the other young and inexperienced, looking to him for guidance as Nicolas approached.

Rhea and Ariana found a place near the main door where Michael was waiting for them, and they could see John and Phaedra Karous is at the other side, but there was no sign of Daphne or her mother.

They will be with Nicolas, Rhea thought. Guests of honour.

Then, suddenly, Nicolas was standing before the great main door with the two priests and his mother by his side.

Alexandra Metaxas had drawn all eyes towards her. Dressed in a flowing silk gown, her titian hair piled high on her head and draped with a magnificent silk shawl in the deep, subtle colours which suited her so

well, she looked magnificent. Rhea saw her in profile
for a moment, thinking how alike mother and son were,
and then Alexandra came towards her, holding out
both hands in spontaneous greeting.

'My child,' she said, 'I have been looking for you
everywhere! Where have you been hiding yourself?'

A warm tide of sensitive colour stained Rhea's cheeks
as they looked into each other's eyes.

'I—took the necklet to the museum.' Rhea could tell
her nothing but the truth. 'I knew Nicolas would wish it
to be there today.'

Alexandra drew her gently forward.

'You must stand with me,' she said. 'It would be
Nicos's wish.'

'Oh, no! Surely——'

Nicolas had turned, seeing them together.

'We are ready to begin,' he said.

Standing there on the sun-dazzled steps of the
museum with Alexandra's fingers closing determinedly
on her elbow, Rhea could neither think nor reason as a
great surge of happiness rose in her heart, blotting out
everything but the memory of her father and his love
for this beautiful land. The two *papas* stood beside
Alexandra as Nicolas handed her the golden key with
which she would open the heavy door.

Alexandra Metaxas did everything with dignity,
stepping back as soon as the door swung open to allow
the assembled villagers and her invited guests a first
view of the magnificent interior. Then, once again, her
hand was under Rhea's elbow, leading her forward
towards the far wall where the veiled plaque had yet to
be uncovered.

People surged behind them, chattering and laughing
in typical Hellenistic fashion as the culmination of the
ceremony approached. The plaque was important to
them as it was to Nicolas, and they were anxious for a
first glimpse of it to see what it said.

It was some time before everyone had filed into the
hall, and Rhea found herself looking for a first sign of
Daphne. When she did see her cousin at last, she was
with her mother, holding Evadne securely by the arm as

they followed Phaedra and John Karousis through the main door.

We should have been together, Rhea thought. My place was by my grandfather's side and Daphne should have been here.

No such thought of propriety had entered John Karousis's head, apparently. He came forward to kiss her on both cheeks, his dark eyes glowing with a gentle pride.

'This is a great day for us all,' he said. 'We are very happy.'

Rhea bent to kiss her grandmother's wrinkled cheek.

'Would you like to sit down?' she asked. 'You have been standing in the sun for over an hour.'

Phaedra shook her head.

'I am well protected,' she said, pulling the black hat forward a little. 'I also am happy for today.'

It was as much as she could manage, but her English was certainly improving and the warmth in her voice had reflected her husband's gentle pride. Everyone was happy, Rhea thought, but where was Daphne? Her cousin, who had been walking in John Karousis's wake, was nowhere to be seen. Evadne, too, had disappeared, spirited away by her determined daughter to another vantage point or even to stand beside Daphne when she eventually pulled the golden cord to reveal the plaque and its message to the waiting assembly.

The noise and confusion of talk and laughter seemed to grow with each passing minute, mounting in a vast crescendo of sound to the arched ceiling and the magnificent frescoes along the walls until the older *papas* held up an admonishing hand. Silence descended on the assembled guests like a blanket, the deep silence of reverence in the presence of a beloved priest as he turned towards Alexandra to take her by the hand. Graciously he led her forward till they were directly in front of the plaque, speaking a few words in his native tongue and then in English, which entirely surprised Rhea since most of the assembled guests were Greek. It was, however, the sort of thing she might have expected from this hospitable, happy, uninhibited race who did nothing by half and welcomed the stranger within its gates with widely extended arms.

She did not know what to do, whether to retreat as unobtrusively as possible or just to stand there a few paces ahead of the crowd waiting for Alexandra to draw the purple velvet curtains and reveal the plaque. In that moment it seemed that everyone was looking at her, wondering who she was, and in that moment too she saw Nicolas again, sternly protective as he stood by his mother's side.

Alexandra reached up, her strong fingers fastening on the golden cord as she pulled the curtains apart and stepped back to read the inscription with a small, almost rueful smile curving her sensitive lips.

Momentarily dazzled by the brightness of the polished brass, it took Rhea several minutes before she was able to appreciate the full meaning of the inscription carved into the stone-mounted plaque.

THE METAXAS-LANGFORD MUSEUM she read, her heart beating so wildly that she felt it must surely be heard even above the cheers. Nicolas had honoured her father as well as his own!

In the hubbub of greetings and speculation which followed she seemed completely alone until John Karousis came to stand beside her.

'Grandpapa!' she said. 'Did you know?'

He nodded, looking round for Phaedra.

'It was a great secret,' he admitted, 'but Nicolas said it was only right that your father should share in the honour because he had worked so selflessly on the initial dig, and Alexandra agreed with him.'

'She is a wonderful person,' Rhea said. 'She could so easily have resented such a gesture to the distant past before she married Nicolas's father.'

'Alexandra would never hold a grudge,' he said. 'She has always been our good friend. But here comes Nicolas,' he added with a twinkle in his eye, 'to ask you what you think of the dedication.'

Nicolas had detached himself from the small group around the plaque and was coming towards them.

'Well,' he demanded, 'are we agreed?'

'I—it was a wonderful gesture,' Rhea told him in a shaken whisper. '*Efharistó*, Nicolas! I can't tell you how much I appreciate what you have done.'

He looked beyond her, as if he was indeed gazing into the past.

'How could it be otherwise,' he said, 'when they worked to closely together on the excavations and your father found the original torque?' His jaw hardened a little. 'It was a tremendous find and he could have lost his life, apparently, when a wall collapsed while he was working. I've spent a lot of time trying to trace it over the years, but now you have restored it to its rightful place in the museum it will be the first thing people will see.'

'The love token!' Rhea mused beneath her breath.

'I mean to use it as a frontispiece to our catalogue,' he told her before he was called away. 'I think it is a fitting emblem for a small museum.'

She saw him several times after that, but never alone. He was an efficient host, conducting the curators of several other museums round the show-cases without forgetting the humble people of the *hora* who had come to share his joy. They had spread out tables in the narrow street behind the museum with green and black olives, pistachio nuts and large bowls of *kalamarákia* and *xiphiòs*, the little swordfish squares skewered with tomato, onion and bay leaf, and there was lamb roasted over a charcoal grill and kebabs of meat to be dipped into a strong garlic sauce before the desserts. The first strawberries had been gathered into huge blue bowls by the young girls who served them, smiling coyly at the fishermen as they filed past, and cherries, red and blushing, in huge baskets lay beside piles of yellow peaches and the yellow-fleshed melons of the Argos. The cheeses had a section to themselves—*fetá* and *kaseri* and a soft white goat cheese eaten with honey.

Rhea met Ariana as she stood at the end of the long table, contemplating a selection of sticky Turkish cakes which appeared to be the ultimate highlight of the feast.

'You'll love them!' she declared, licking her fingers appreciatively as she demolished yet another sticky

helping of flaky pastry, honey and nuts. 'And they are
very good for you! Have you seen Daphne?' she added
almost as an afterthought.

Rhea shook her head.

'Not since Kyria Metaxas unveiled the plaque.'

'Daphne thought she was going to do it, but Nicolas
didn't ask her. I wonder why, because she was so sure
that he would.' Ariana drained her glass of lemonade.
'Michael is taking us back in the caique before it gets
dark,' she added, 'but perhaps Nicolas has asked you to
stay?'

'Why should he?' Rhea asked. 'He has other guests to
consider.'

'Most of them will be returning to Athens. It's been a
wonderful day!' Ariana declared.

Already some of the assembled guests were beginning
to leave, piling into the yachts and motor launches
which lay along the mole, but the sun was still high and
the spell of the island held them in its gentle grasp.
Michael came to sit beside them, sipping a final glass of
wine.

'Your father and Nicolas's father must have been
very close,' he mused. 'I think we sometimes under-
estimate our parents, believing that we have the
monopoly of emotion, but it looks as if they were very
good friends at one time. Anyway, their two names will
always be there together on the plaque, and that should
make you feel very proud.'

Rhea could hardly answer him. All her love for her
father had welled to the surface again and she knew
that she would never be able to repay Nicolas for what
he had done; yet there was no real way of expressing
her gratitude other than thanking him for the gesture he
had made.

As the crowd thinned she could see Daphne and her
mother moving slowly among the last of his guests and
finally her cousin came to stand beside them.

'It's been a most exciting day,' she said. 'Have you
enjoyed yourself?' Her tone was coolly confident, as if
she had indeed taken over the role of Nicolas's hostess.
'I think the village people did us proud, don't you? All

that wonderful food and drink! It was quite lavish and
Nicolas certainly appreciated it. Of course, they will
benefit greatly from the museum in the summer months
once it becomes a tourist attraction and that will help to
keep the younger ones from rushing off to Athens or
one of the larger islands to find work. The families of
the *hora* are very closely knit, like most Greek families,'
she added, speaking directly to Rhea for the first time.
'I gather you'll be going back to Volponé with
Grandmama and Grandpapa. Nicolas mentioned that
he had asked Michael to take you in the caique as far as
Piraeus.' She glanced across at her mother. 'We won't
be going,' she explained with evident satisfaction.
'Nicolas has offered us accommodation overnight with
some other special guests—Ida and Philip Xilas and
Jason Papadam and Paris, who is anxious to come back
to work on the excavations—so we'll be at the villa, I
expect.'

Wondering if Alexandra Metaxas would also stay or
if she would sail back to the mainland in Nicolas's
caique, Rhea turned to find Evadne by her side.

'Have you enjoyed yourself, Aunt Evadne?' she asked
automatically. 'Everything seems to have gone so well.'

'Indeed it has,' Evadne said. 'I didn't want to come,
but now I am glad that I did.' She watched her
daughter's progress as Daphne moved confidently
among the remaining guests. 'Now that he has
established the museum on Norbos Nicolas will have
time to think of other things,' she added. 'He and
Daphne will soon marry, and that will be justification
for all I have done for her all my life. It will be the
union of two Greek families who should have been
joined together long ago.'

Rhea knew that her aunt's words were an oblique
reference to her mother and Nicolas's father who were
engaged to be married when Charles Langford came on
the scene and 'stole Maria away', as Phaedra Karousis
herself had once said, and she was aware of the bitterness
and pride in her stern-faced aunt as she spoke of the
future. But why should Evadne care so much? Was it
only her deeply rooted sense of Greek unity which

made her so adamant, or was there a more personal reason for Evadne's hostility?

Alexandra Metaxas came with Nicolas to say goodbye.

'I've decided to stay till tomorrow,' she told them, 'when Michael will bring the caique back here to collect us.'

She had made no direct reference to Daphne or Evadne, but at least she would also be on the island, Rhea thought as she shook hands with Nicolas before boarding the caique.

'Thank you for everything,' he said almost formally before they sailed away.

Rhea stood on the deck alone, watching as Norbos faded in the last of the sunlight until it was no more than a green speck on the turquoise-coloured sea. This might be the last time she would ever see it, the last farewell.

They rounded Sounion just before sunset as the amazing violet light spread from the crest of Mount Hymettus across the whole Attic plain, throwing a warm glow over the flanks of the mountain and the vine country beyond. Its radiance enveloped everything for a moment, and then, as if a switch had been pressed by the hand of some Olympian deity, the light had gone and everything had turned a dull, uniform grey and the mountain magic was engulfed in the shadows of the coming night.

The north wind blew coldly against her cheek as she turned away, thinking that Greece itself had abandoned her, but one thing she did know was that she had left part of herself behind on Norbos, where Nicolas had remained with her cousin Daphne.

CHAPTER SEVEN

IN her aunt's absence Rhea helped Ariana in the house the following morning. The long day on Norbos had tired Phaedra Karousis more than she realised and they had persuaded her to sleep late, but John Karousis had gone early to the vineyard to inspect a new planting machine which had just arrived and they decided to hurry through their work and climb up to Florina for a swim before the soporific, sundazzled hour of noon.

Rhea was first downstairs, and it seemed a long time before Ariana followed her to the terrace where their coffee was waiting for them.

'Come on!' she called through the silent hall. 'I'm dying for a swim.'

Ariana came slowly towards her from the terrace door like a sleepwalker, her eyes wide and bright with tension as she placed something on the table between them.

'I found this,' she said, her voice no more than a whisper. 'It is the replica of the torque you brought from England. I found it in Aunt Evadne's room when I went to replace her ironing in her drawer.'

Rhea could hardly believe her eyes as she gazed down at the necklet lying on the marble-topped table. Was it—could it be—her own necklet? Her hands trembled and her whole body seemed to shake as she picked it up, remembering something which she had entirely forgotten until now. A tiny semi-precious stone had been missing from the clasp of the neck ornament her father had given her and for a moment she could hardly look at the gold clasp sparkling in the slant of sunlight which poured down through the vines.

'What is it?' Ariana asked. 'What is wrong?'

'There was a stone missing on the clasp,' Rhea said. 'I forgot about it before——'

Her eyes were on the necklet, seeing the place where

the tiny stone had been, seeing the empty setting which had once held it in place as if it encompassed her entire world. Here was the truth! Her father's memory still remained bright and shining before her, and she could go to Norbos and show Nicolas the proof of the older man's integrity!

Yet what was the use? She had put the real torque back in the museum where it belonged, and he was going to marry Daphne.

'Ariana,' she said harshly, 'can we keep this a secret for now? I don't want anyone to know. Just you and I.'

The love token her father had given her, the neck ornament fashioned so carefully all those years ago by an Athenian craftsman, was hers to keep while the original torque was restored to Nicolas to treasure in his island museum for ever. All things being equal, she should have no more room for regret, yet regret followed her unremittingly to culminate in a wild despair. How could she remain at Volponé with Nicolas and Daphne so near?

The following morning she locked her own necklet safely away in her suitcase before she went down to the terrace, but she could not discuss the original torque or the fact that Evadne must have taken it long ago and used it when the occasion arrived, to discredit the niece from England whom she couldn't love, so that her own daughter might marry Nicolas.

When she was alone with John Karousis, at last, Rhea said quietly,

'Grandpapa, I must go. I have been so happy here with you, but I must go back to my own country.'

She would not look into the kind old eyes she knew would be full of concern and disappointment, keeping her own eyes on the splash of sunlight which dazzled the marble table-top through the vines.

'But you are part of Greece now,' John Karousis objected. 'You are one of us.'

She shook her head, afraid of the tears she might shed at such a parting.

'We want you to stay.' He put a gentle hand over

hers. 'We cannot let you go so soon! We do not want you to go at all.'

'I must.' She rose to her feet, the tears choking her. 'You see, it was just a little holiday, Grandpapa, a—week or two to get to know you.'

'And you do not think it has been good, getting to know us?' he queried uncertainly.

'Oh, Grandpapa!' She turned towards him, the tears shed at last. 'It has been—like a dream I have had for a long time. It has been everything I've ever hoped for. If only I could let you know how much it has meant to me—just belonging!'

'But you tell me you wish to go, and I do not understand why unless you can tell me.'

Rhea turned her head aside. How could she tell him that she could not stay in his fair country loving Nicolas so much?

'I can't,' she said in a shaken whisper. 'It's something I can't explain, even to you.'

His fingers tightened their grip on her hand as she looked down into his understanding eyes.

'You will come back one day,' he said, 'because you belong here.'

She belonged, it was true, Rhea thought, but she would never come back.

For a long time they walked in the garden with the scent of stocks and roses heavy on the air, and the thickets of pink and white oleanders hedging them in. It was a quiet place for their reverie at that time of day when the morning's work was finished and the siesta hour had not begun, but something had happened to the peace she had always found there. When they halted in the shade of a mulberry tree to look out over the olive grove she gazed back at the house as if to say good-bye, seeing it almost submerged in creepers and hibiscus, and so still that it seemed to be listening.

She would always think of it that way, a haunt of ancient peace, with the drone of bees in the honeysuckle and the blinding sun of midday dazzling the pristine beauty of marble terrace walls.

When they had finally circled the house and walked

as far as the *stoa*, John Karousis sat down in his accustomed chair, glad of the shade the open portico afforded as he lit his pipe.

'You will think again about what you have said,' he suggested, 'but I will not press you to stay at Volponé if your heart is in some other place.'

Rhea put her hand on his shoulder for a moment.

'It will always be here,' she said, 'but I must go.'

She turned from him, her fingers fastening on the golden torque at her throat which had started it all, the love token which had betrayed her into loving for a second time, although this had been different. Nicolas had never protested his love for her and she had given hers without question. It had been as inevitable as the dawn rising above the mists around Mount Dirfis or the sun going down beyond the twin peaks of Parnassos, something over which she had no control.

She had never been able to sleep in the middle of the day, but she went to her room after their light lunch of fruit and cheese, standing before the window for a long time to look out across the garden and the chestnut trees to the encircling mountains beyond, green now in the full glare of sunlight. The changing face of these mountains would always remind her of Greece and the short time she had lived here at Volponé as part of John Karousis's family.

The sound of a car's wheels crunching across the gravel beneath her window alerted her to the fact that they had a visitor, and her foolish heart quickened its beat as she looked down for Nicolas's familiar grey convertible. Instead, she saw her aunt standing there dressed in the sombre black suit and straw hat which she had worn at the opening ceremony on Norbos two days ago. Evadne was clutching a small overnight bag and Rhea supposed that it belonged to Daphne, almost expecting to see her cousin alighting from the hired car in her mother's wake.

Evadne, however, was alone. She marched into the house as if something had upset her while the taxi driver followed with a large suitcase which, by the expensive look of it, could be no other than Daphne's.

Had mother and daughter quarrelled, Rhea wondered, or was this just Daphne's way of making use of everybody in sight when she had decided to change her plans? Decided, perhaps, to go off with Nicolas at a moment's notice?

Her aunt's heavy footfall sounded on the treads of the stairs, mounting to her own room at the far end of the corridor, and then silence reigned once more.

The quiet house came back to vigorous life at three o'clock when Yianni roused the other servants and set about his tasks for the afternoon. Sometimes he worked among the vines, sometimes he chopped wood or fetched charcoal for the kitchen, but in spite of his many years he was always busy. He survived the sharp edge of Evadne's tongue with a philosophic smile in the sure knowledge that John Karousis would never dismiss him no matter how loudly she complained, and it seemed that Evadne had accepted the situation over the years.

She was directing his efforts with the charcoal grill when Rhea went slowly down the staircase to stand at the open kitchen door.

'Have you enjoyed your short holiday, Aunt Evadne?' she asked conversationally. 'The opening ceremony went off very well, I thought.'

Evadne turned at the sound of her voice, her gaze fastening immediately on the torque, and for a moment she looked completely disconcerted.

'But—you gave it to the museum,' she objected.

'Not this one.' Rhea's fingers closed on the necklet at her throat. 'This is mine, Aunt Evadne. It always was. It is the copy I brought with me from London, but I think you know that.' She drew a deep breath. 'What I can't understand,' she said, 'is why you took it and put the real one in my room so that I would stand accused in Nicolas's eyes. But you needn't have bothered,' she added desperately. 'He was never in love with me.'

Evadne took a step towards her.

'No,' she managed. 'It is Daphne he should marry by right—one of his own race. Your father came here long ago and took my sister to England and our family, who had suffered many losses by war, lost a daughter also.' She drew herself up to her full, commanding height, her confidence suddenly restored. 'Daphne and Nicolas will be married when she returns from Rome,' she added dramatically. 'She will only remain there for a few days to model some clothes and then she will return to Athens with her own trousseau.'

Rhea's immediate reaction was to rush from the room, but she was forced to ask,

'Where did you get the original necklet—the torque?'

Her aunt hesitated, reluctant to be questioned in such a way, and then she answered truthfully enough.

'I took it when your father left it here to be returned to Kostas Metaxas for the museum he had planned to set up on Norbos.' She drew a deep breath before she plunged on to explain. 'I had nothing of value in my life when I was widowed after Daphne was born, and I took it for her in case she never married. I was mad— yes,' she allowed in a rare moment of truth, 'but I had to do it. I had nothing else to give her.'

They stood gazing at each other for a moment, face to face without pretence, until Rhea turned away.

'It is best forgotten,' she said harshly. 'There is no point in making an issue of it now.'

Evadne followed her on to the terrace. 'What will you do?' she asked.

'Do?' Rhea shrugged her shoulders. 'I will do nothing, Aunt Evadne. I am going back to England and I don't want to cause trouble for anyone in the meantime.'

To her utter surprise her aunt's eyes filled with tears. They were difficult tears for a woman of her age who had often been acquainted with grief and had schooled herself not to show it.

'I thank you,' she said. 'I thank you with all my heart. If he found out what I did my father would never forgive me, and I depend on him now. He would brand me a thief.'

The situation had been saved as far as she was concerned, and her relief was obvious. Bereft of

Volponé's shelter, where else could she go with her limited knowledge of the world and her lack of everything but a domestic training? Rhea didn't believe for one moment that John Karousis would cast her out—he was far too kind and too generous for that— but Evadne was evidently afraid of his wrath.

Keeping her distance after that initial display of gratitude, her aunt was still watchful and still prepared to criticise, going about her household tasks with the same determination to express her martyrdom, although she did not speak about the necklet again or refer to the day they had spent on Norbos at the opening of the museum. If Nicolas had escorted Daphne to Rome afterwards she did not say so, leaving Rhea to draw her own conclusions in that respect, and all that Rhea could think about was the fact that he had not yet returned to Florina.

The temperature had soared into the eighties during the past few days, making the atmosphere hot and sticky by midday, and they had spent two afternoons at Florina swimming in the pool and resting in the shade of the house before they walked back through the olive grove in the late afternoon to help with the evening meal. On both occasions the house had looked deserted, although Semele had appeared on the second afternoon with a tray bearing orange juice, *visináda* and the sticky preserved fruits Ariana liked so much.

'Michael promised to phone,' she said as they sat on the terrace tying on their shoes for the return journey to Volponé. 'He said he would let me know about his new caique, but he must be too busy with work.' She heaved a small, regretful sigh. 'He might even forget altogether,' she added dolefully. 'Young men are so unreliable when they suddenly have a new toy to play with. He has wanted his own boat ever since he came back from America, but he did promise to take us sailing for a whole day among the Islands. You'd like that, Rhea, wouldn't you—a sort of final trip round the Cyclades before you return to England?'

'I don't know. I don't think there will be time,' Rhea said, getting to her feet to avoid looking at her cousin.

'A week isn't very long, especially when someone is buying a boat.'

She had tried to speak lightly about her decision to go, but the words came out drenched in sorrow.

'You don't want to go!' Ariana exclaimed. 'I knew it. You are going because something has upset you. Was it Aunt Evadne?'

'No.' Rhea's voice was none too steady. 'You know that I only came for a holiday to meet everybody and—to see Volponé for myself.'

'But that was before you grew to love it so much,' her cousin protested. 'Something must have happened—something must have made you change your mind. You said only a few days ago that you could live here for ever.'

'We say these things on the spur of the moment, Ari, without really meaning them.'

'*You* don't!' Ariana was on her feet, challenging her with accusing eyes. 'You said you had fallen in love with Greece, and it is *half* your country, so why should you want to leave it so quickly? Volponé could be your home for as long as you need it. Grandpapa has said so and he will be very sad when you go away.'

'I know.' Rhea looked back at Florina sleeping peacefully in the sun. 'Everyone has been so kind and I feel so ungrateful, but I have to go.'

'You are really unhappy about leaving us,' Ariana said. 'I do not understand. If you love everything here, why must you go away?' She picked up her towelling jacket from the sun-lounger. 'Is it because of Nicolas?' she asked.

Rhea walked a few paces in the sunshine.

'Nicolas is going to marry Daphne,' she cried harshly.

'Oh—I wish it was *you*!' her cousin cried. 'He will not be happy with her, I know. Nicos deserves better than that. She is so selfish and dedicated to her career. She will not make a good wife for him. Not at all! He needs someone like his mother, someone who loves Greece and will want to stay here.'

'We don't know what Daphne will be like once

they're married,' Rhea said. 'She might be—everything he desires.'

'I doubt it! She'll go off to Rome, or Paris, or New York at the drop of a hat to convince herself that she is still at the top of her profession. and Nicos won't be able to do a thing about it. She's not at all good with children, you know, and Nicos will have a desire for a family, like all Greek men. They love especially little girls who are able to wrap them in their little fingers!'

'"Twist them round their little finger".' Rhea tried to laugh. 'As you do your grandfather,' she reminded her cousin, steering the conversation away from Nicolas and his marriage to Daphne.

'Yes, that is so,' Ariana agreed, 'but they are also very proud of their sons. Nicos must hope for a son to carry on his name—many sons, perhaps—and a daughter to spoil.' She heaved a deep sigh. 'It is all so very sad,' she declared.

They had come to the olive grove which divided Florina from Volponé, and Rhea looked back for the last time, but she was unable to see the house because of its surrounding trees, and the sun had already cast shadows on the far side of the valley where the mountains rose starkly against the sky.

When they reached Volponé a tall man was standing on the edge of the terrace looking out across the vineyards as he waited for their return. His face was in shadow and for one brief moment Rhea's heart seemed to stand still, but it was Michael who came swiftly towards them.

'I was on my way back to Athens,' he explained. 'I've been up to my eyes in work for the past few days.'

'I thought you were buying a yacht,' Ariana tried to say coldly. 'That would have been as good an excuse as any for not phoning as you promised.'

'I did manage to buy a yacht,' he agreed, 'but the other excuse is really quite genuine, Ari. You know what my father is like—business before pleasure has always been his motto and this was quite a tough assignment. I had to do battle with several people older than myself, but he didn't take their ages or experience into account. He has always believed in the old Spartan adage: "Come back with your shield—or on it!" so that's why I delayed so long.'

Ariana's look softened.

'What have you done with the new boat?' she demanded.

'Left it at Mikrolimano at the Yacht Club.' He grinned down at her. 'You won't have long to wait till your curiosity is satisfied because I'm bringing it round to Karistos tomorrow to take you sailing for a whole day. I've already asked your grandfather,' he added to defeat all argument.

Arian's nose was no longer in the air, suggesting her indifference.

'You are inviting Rhea, too, of course,' she said.

'Of course!'

'Perhaps it will make her change her mind,' Ariana suggested. 'She's preparing to go back to London.'

'Surely not?' Michael said gallantly. 'We would miss you too much.' He walked with them along the terrace. 'You will come, though, even if it is only to say goodbye to the Cyclades?'

'Yes.' Rhea hid her eyes with her hand, brushing back her hair. 'It is very kind of you, Michael.'

'And you are very brave to come out on the caique's maiden voyage,' he responded, 'but I do assure you I am an experienced navigator, since I have sailed many times with Nicolas.'

'How is he?' Rhea's voice was steady now. 'We haven't seen him since the museum was opened, but perhaps he has—gone away on business.'

'I don't think so,' Michael said. 'I saw him in Athens this morning. He was in Stadiou, buying shirts.'

So Nicolas was not in Rome, after all, although that didn't mean he was not going to marry Daphne. A girl wouldn't want her fiancé there when she was buying her trousseau!

'Are you going to stay for supper?' Ariana was asking, having completely forgiven Michael for not phoning as he had promised.

'I only wish I could,' he said regretfully, 'but I have

to report back to the office where my father will be waiting. If I'm to have a full day off to take you sailing tomorrow I must account for myself this evening, but I think the deal I've made should please him.'

'You make a Big Bad Wolf out of him when he is really a darling!' Ariana accused. 'He would grant you any favour.'

'You make it all sound far too easy!' he grinned. 'See you tomorrow at eleven o'clock—and don't be late!'

'I never am,' Ariana lied charmingly.

They were at the south end of the peninsula long before eleven o'clock the following morning, but Michael was already there, waiting and eager to show off his new possession.

'Come aboard,' he said, appearing on deck in a startling blue-and-red sweater and a pair of blue jeans. 'We had a good trip round Sounion early this morning and made record time.' He glanced at the northern sky. 'It's clouding over a bit, but it should clear eventually. Can I give you a hand?'

He stretched up to help Rhea, seeing the sudden pallor of her face as she looked back at the mountains she had come to love and might be leaving soon for ever.

'Is anything wrong?' he asked quietly.

'No—nothing. It's just—rather sad to be saying goodbye.'

'I know how you feel.' He held her hand in a tight grip. 'When I left for New York two years ago I thought I was going for good, and it was like a death sentence.'

'But you're back now,' she said, 'to stay.'

'I hope so,' he agreed. 'I could never really settle anywhere else.'

Walking along the deck she could feel the sudden motion of the water under her feet and the surge of it along the hull, and it seemed as if she had only to look up to find Nicolas, strong and reassuring, at the helm.

Well, he wasn't here, she told herself, and that was the end of it. There was no reason why she should spoil her last day among the Islands in useless regret. It would hardly be fair to Ariana or Michael either, who

had made such an effort to please her, but everywhere
she looked there was another memory. When they set
sail there were the busy cargo steamers plying their way
to the larger islands and farther afield to the
Dardanelles and Samos and Kos, while all around them
the scattered Cyclades rose dramatically from the sea,
their mountain peaks shimmering in the sunshine, their
golden beaches beckoning as they passed.

The sun had come out in full strength again, dancing
on the water, and a couple of dolphins followed them
playfully for over half-an-hour before they veered away
towards Andros and the open sea.

Rhea studied the chart Michael had given her,
looking for the tiny dot which was Norbos on the vast
expanse of water, and finding it eventually when they
were almost upon it.

'Are we going in?' Ariana asked. 'It would be lots of
fun!'

Rhea's heart seemed to stand still as she waited for
Michael's decision.

'Perhaps on the way back,' he said after a moment's
consideration. 'I'd like to go as far as Tinos, though
part of it will be open sea. It will all depend on the
wind,' he decided.

There were other yachts tacking around them
towards the island of their choice, large and small, with
white sails billowing or engines chugging powerfully to
speed them on their way. The water was like emerald
glass touched here and there by their lengthening
wakes, and always on the horizon another mountain
peak rose to beckon them on.

They approached Nicolas's island from the north,
sailing past the promontory where the pink-domed
church stood out conspicuously against the sky and the
bare hillsides dropped gradually to the sea. The *hora*
and its small, sheltered harbour faced south, but they
came parallel with it eventually, seeing it in full sunlight,
the white cubic houses rising one above the other as
they climbed the slope to the plateau and the villa
among the cypress trees.

Foolishly Rhea expected to see Nicolas standing

there, but the island looked curiously deserted. Only when they came abreast of the harbour entrance did they see the large motor yacht moored along the mole, as it had been two days ago when the museum was first opened.

'It looks as if Philip Xilas has decided to stay for good!' Michael remarked. 'Paris is very keen, I think, and would like to spend more time at the dig. Nicolas has a host of willing helpers!'

Was Daphne also there? Rhea looked away from the sleepy mole to the open sea and back again to the lovely island where she had surely left her heart. 'Good-bye!' she whispered under her breath. 'Good-bye, my love!'

They sailed on until the hired deck hand brought a meal from the tiny galley to the well, where they sat round munching crisp bread rolls spread with *taramasaláta* and canapés of *brik* washed down down with *mastíka*, the sweet, faintly scented wine Rhea had come to like. It was all so relaxed and tranquil as the sails billowed out above them and the waves ran smoothly along the hull.

Then, with amazing alacrity, Michael was on his feet, passing the tiller to the hired hand to run quickly along the deck in his bare feet.

The foresail came down with a quiver, like a frightened bird, and for the first time Rhea became aware that the sun was not so bright. Away to the north the mountains looked black and ominous while the sea ahead of them had turned from blue to grey. Out of nowhere a strong wind began to blow and Ariana looked concerned.

'Surely it is too early for the *meltémi*?' she breathed. 'We never get it before August, as a rule.'

The sky was darkening almost by the minute, as if a great cloak had been thrown across the Islands, obscuring them one by one.

'It's a storm,' Ariana said. 'A bad one——'

Michael came back along the deck with a grim look in his eyes.

'Are we going to be caught?' Ariana asked. 'I hate the sea when it looks like this!'

'We'll be all right.' Michael had put as much assurance into the calming words as he could. 'I'm going to turn round.'

'We could go back to Norbos,' Ariana suggested helpfully.

'Yes.' He put the mainsail over, pulling the boom in as it swung across. 'We must find shelter of some sort before this breaks.'

The storm appeared to be rushing towards them, tearing at the sail and churning the waves into a wild froth of foam along the hull until it seemed more than he could do to hold to the course he had set. Rhea sat very still, remembering that caiques were not very reliable boats in a bad sea, remembering Nicolas's criticism of his own yacht which was much bigger than this one. The smiling blue Aegean had been churned into an angry grey maelstrom of tossing water, and she soon realised that they were in difficulty as the unexpected wind blew strongly against them. They were driven before it, flying helplessly along at an alarming speed as Michael struggled powerfully with the sail and the hired hand steered with his teeth clenched and his bare feet braced against the gunwale to give him added strength.

When the sail came down the brave little caique seemed to stagger in her tracks, but the engine barked into life reassuringly as Michael pulled in the slack, strapping the billowing nylon to the boom where it flapped alarmingly for a moment before they moved on. Even as they heaved a first sigh of relief, however, they were conscious of the wind pawing at them, reluctant to let them go.

Michael said between his teeth.

'It's Norbos or bust! We can't go all the way back to the mainland on the engine. We just haven't got enough fuel.'

The little yacht reared and bucked at the waves, ploughing into them one minute, riding them the next, sending flying spume across the foredeck like a flapping shroud to the accompaniment of the wind in the rigging and the snarl of the angry sea. It was as if a thousand

demons had sprung up from nowhere to attack them
with all the destructive fury at their command, but
Rhea held her breath, determined not to show her fear.
With Tinos and Andros already out of sight, their
mountains enveloped in a grey blanket of obscurity,
there was nothing for it but to plunge ahead. Michael
apparently knew what he was doing, and George, the
deck-hand, was also an experienced sailor, so apart
from an accident, they would reach their destination
safely enough.

And that destination was Norbos! She was going
back almost against her will to the island where she had
bid her love farewell.

She saw Ariana biting her lip in an effort not to panic
as Michael laid a reassuring hand on her arm.

'Not long now,' he said. 'We'll soon be there!'

Knowing so little about boats or engines, it was some
time before Rhea acknowledged the fact that he was
having trouble with the caique. George had gone below
to appear again with a canvas bag of tools and he lay
on the floor of the wheelhouse for a long time before he
came back into the well.

'Best to go down now,' he advised in his halting
English so that Rhea would understand. 'Rain will
come soon. You will get wet.'

They were wet enough as it was, Rhea thought, with
the spray rising high over the foredeck to flood back
towards them in a deluge of salt water which had now
settled around their feet. Ariana had made an effort
with the pump but it had evidently defeated her.

'We couldn't be more wet than we are,' she said,
shivering a little. 'I'll stay here.'

Michael appeared at the door of the wheelhouse.

'Go down and try to dry yourself out,' he
commanded, 'then get as many blankets as you can
find—to keep yourself warm,' he added almost as an
afterthought. 'You could also try to make some cocoa.
It will keep the chill at bay.'

Aware that he might be trying to hide his own
anxiety, Rhea went below without argument, but
Ariana lingered to ask some other question.

'I don't like it when Michael gets all uptight like that,' she announced when she finally descended to the cabin where Rhea had set out a tray with the utmost difficulty. 'I think we're in trouble.'

'Maybe the storm will blow itself out.' Rhea caught one of the mugs as it whizzed past her across the polished table. 'Talk about "all hands on deck",' she added. 'I'm glad you came down to offer me an extra pair here!'

'You're bluffing!' Ariana accused her. 'You're as scared as I am.'

'Of course I'm scared, but I trust Michael. He really is experienced,' Rhea said. 'Can you steady the kettle while I try to light the stove?'

'Cocoa makes me sick,' Ariana announced.

'Well—have we any tea?'

'No. There's coffee—I'll make it black and strong.'

Airana reached for the jar only to be thrown sideways on to the nearest bunk while Rhea saved herself by grabbing the edge of the table as a second wave struck them broadside on.

'Have you noticed anything?' Ariana gasped, straightening up to retrieve the coffee jar. 'There isn't any sound.'

'What about all that noise out there—wind and waves?'

'I meant the engine.' Ariana was already at the foot of the short companionway leading to the deck. 'It's stopped.'

Rhea pulled her back.

'George was seeing to it. He was doing something with all those tools.'

'Not enough!' Ariana shook herself free. 'I'm going up to see what it's all about.'

When she reappeared the caique seemed to be wallowing in a deep trough, swinging from side to side.

'The engine has given up,' she said in an almost casual tone. 'We're drifting. There's been a lull in the storm—a temporary one—so we have to hope for the best. I'll get the blankets.'

Automatically Rhea prepared cocoa and coffee in two separate jugs, aware that she felt very little in this unexpected crisis. Ariana's moment of panic had also passed in her search for sufficient blankets which she passed up on deck to George.

The wind had gone down but the greyness still remained as they climbed back on to the deck. They had been longer on the storm-tossed caique than she realised and it would soon be dark, with the sudden nightfall adding to their difficulties.

George was still at work on the recalcitrant engine while Michael sat in the wheelhouse peering into the surrounding gloom as if he might dispel it with a look.

'We're not going to get out of this too easily,' he confided to Rhea when she offered him a mug of hot cocoa. 'I've sent out a distress signal, but so far I've had no reply. Everyone must have scuttled for safety as soon as they saw the clouds gathering.'

'The wind has died down a bit,' Rhea said encouragingly.

'Yes.' He did not qualify the brief acknowledgment and she wondered why. 'Have you found enough blankets?' he asked.

'It depends on how many we're likely to need.'

He hesitated.

'We could feel the cold during the night.' He looked directly into her eyes. 'I don't expect this present lull to last very long.'

'Where exactly are we?' She felt cold now, but not because of the wind.

He pushed the chart towards her, indicating a spot with his forefinger.

'Off the direct shipping lane, I'm afraid. Don't alarm Ariana, though. We could still be picked up.'

Darkness fell and the wind rose again, although with much less fury. They appeared to be carried steadily across the water instead of being buffeted in every direction, but an eternity seemed to pass before anyone spoke. Ariana had distributed the four blankets she had found, but nobody used them because they were still sheltered enough huddled together in the wheelhouse, gazing out at nothing. Then, suddenly, George got swiftly to his feet to peer out into the darkness. When he turned he spoke to Michael in rapid, excitable Greek.

Rhea saw the knuckles on Michael's hands go white as he gripped the wheel which had almost been torn from his grasp, knowing that they were being carried rapidly towards disaster.

No one spoke. They could see the rocks ahead of them now and the darker cliff face rising almost perpendicular out of the sea, but the caique seemed to come to rest among them almost gently. There was a grating sound as she turned over on her side, like a white bird come to rest on the shore, followed by a lurch backwards as the receding waves pulled her with them.

'We're holding,' Michael said between his teeth. 'We'll have to pull her further up the rocks to safety.'

For the next hour they struggled in wind and rain to establish their advantage, resting only when they could jump ashore for the final effort of easing their disabled craft further on to the rocks which were tearing her apart.

'We'll have to climb higher up,' Michael decided. 'It'll be stiff going, but we must try.' He cast a last, lingering glance at his stranded pride and joy. 'I didn't have her very long, did I?' he said.

'Do you know where we are?' Ariana asked, looking up at the stern rock face confronting them in the darkness.

'More or less. We're this side of Norbos on the rocky spur near the north end of the island. You know the one I mean?'

Ariana nodded.

'About as far away from anywhere as we could be,' she suggested. 'Everything on Norbos faces south—the *hora* and the bay and the church—and the villa and the lodge. Besides,' she added, 'we're not *on* the island where people might look for us, or where we could walk to safety.'

'We'll see what we can do with a flare or two,' Michael promised. 'Meanwhile, we're on dry land and that's a bonus.'

They climbed up the cliff with difficulty, resting on a

ledge which jutted out conveniently with a canopy of rock above it which might afford them shelter from the rain when the wind went down.

'We'll wait here,' Michael said.

Huddled in their respective blankets, they settled down as best they could, setting off the four flares at intervals in the hope of attracting attention, but there was no passing ship to come to their rescue, no answering light to assure them that they had been seen.

They ate the biscuits they had brought from the galley, drinking dark Turkish coffee from a flask, and once or twice Rhea thought that her cousin had fallen asleep. The rain drifted away and stars came out, like bright eyes watching over them in the sky.

'I feel better when I can see the stars,' Ariana murmured. 'There's Orion with his faithful dog, Sirius, and soon we will be able to see the Pole Star and the Plough.'

She had recovered from the fear she had shown on the water and even Michael looked up at the stars.

'We'll stay here,' he said, 'till it gets light. Do you think you can sleep?'

'Where are *you* going?' Ariana demanded suspiciously.

'Down to the caique. I'll have another shot at raising help.'

Someone on Norbos was sure to respond, Rhea thought, someone who would come swiftly to their aid. Nicolas, she wondered, or was he already on the mainland with Daphne?

It didn't seem to matter so much now that all their thoughts were concentrated on getting off the rocks which were tearing the gallant little caique to pieces on the shore below.

It was over an hour before Michael returned.

'I can't raise a whisper,' he admitted. 'The storm seems to have put everybody off the air.' He glanced at his wristwatch. 'It's twelve o'clock. Everyone on Norbos will be asleep by now.'

'Do you think there will be anyone at the dig—in the Lodge, perhaps?' Rhea asked. 'I remember someone playing around with a short-wave transmitter. I think it was Paris.'

'They would have a more powerful one on *Swordfish*,' Michael decided. 'That's what I can't understand. Even if there are no other yachts around *Swordfish* should have picked us up.'

'She was in the harbour when we passed,' Ariana reminded them, 'but they may have made the best of their chances to get back to the mainland.'

'On a yacht like that they could go anywhere,' Michael said. 'I don't like the things, but a powerful engine has its advantages in an emergency.'

'Much better than one that doesn't work at all!' Ariana was trying to make them laugh. 'When you get your insurance claim, Michael, you'll have to settle for a motor launch.'

'Never!' he declared, settling down beside her. 'Have we any more coffee to spare?'

'Half a cupful each, but I'm reserving that for breakfast.' Ariana yawned as she let her head rest on his shoulder. 'I think I might be able to sleep, after all.'

In their far from comfortable positions, crouched on the hard surface of the rock, it was difficult even to doze and the slightest movement brought them back to full consciousness. Now that the northern sky had been washed clear and all the stars were out it was easier to see in the dark, and for a long time Rhea sat watching the water far beneath them for any movement on its surface. She must have fallen into an uneasy sleep eventually, but a quick movement from Michael's direction alerted her again. He had laid the sleeping Ariana aside and was standing on the edge of the ledge peering out across the sea.

'Down there!' he whispered as she struggled to her feet. 'Do you see anything?

'Lights,' Rhea said beneath her breath. 'Two lights——'

'Navigation lights, fore and aft, and another one at the top of a mast!'

She caught his arm.

'Do you think they've seen us?'

'They will see the caique. She's still there, in spite of everything!' He could no longer keep the excitement out of his voice. 'Don't waken the others for a moment,' he cautioned. 'I want to be absolutely sure.'

'What do you think it is?'

'A fishing boat, bound for Norbos, I shouldn't wonder. They could have taken shelter elsewhere during the storm.'

Rhea's heart lifted on a great surge of relief.

'They're moving in!' she exclaimed. 'The lights have changed position—green now nearest us.'

'Waken the others.' He lowered himself over the ledge to find a foothold on the rock below. 'Don't attempt to come down on your own, and don't let Ariana do anything foolish.'

He had gone with the words and she picked up his discarded blanket as George stirred to full consciousness behind her. Ariana slept on, murmuring uncertainly now that she had no comfortable shoulder to lean on.

An eternity of waiting passed as their eyes became more accustomed to the dim light and they could make out the contours of a boat steering its careful way towards the rocks. When it had nearly reached the shore it stopped and they heard the engine going into reverse.

'They have seen us, *thespinis*!' George cried. 'They are coming ashore!'

Ariana was rubbing the sleep out of her eyes.

'Are we saved?' she demanded. 'Has someone come to rescue us?'

'Yes.' Rhea pointed. 'Down there. They must be putting out a dinghy.'

Two dark figures had detached themselves from the deck of the fishing boat and lowered themselves into the tender. Fishermen, Rhea supposed, while all the time she was thinking about Nicolas Metaxas and the purposeful way he seemed to handle every situation.

The men climbed steadily up the cliff, joined now by Michael in his distinguishing white shirt and pale jeans.

'We'll give them a cheer,' Ariana suggested, excitedly. 'They deserve it!'

'Wait till they get here,' Rhea cautioned, feeling very much like cheering herself.

The men were nearly at the ledge, negotiating the last difficult part of the climb, and she knelt on the hard rock to offer a helping hand. Instantly her fingers were gripped in a tight hold.

'Stand back from the edge,' Nicolas commanded in a voice so well-remembered that she could have cried. 'I don't want to hurt you.'

He came up over the edge still holding on to her hand, but there was nothing she could say to him in that overwhelming moment of thankfulness except to repeat his name over and over again.

'Nicolas! Nicolas——!'

'My foolish love!' He folded her in his arms, putting his windcheater about her shoulders as Michael appeared behind him. 'Come home. Come back to Norbos, where you belong!'

Rhea stood quite still, feeling the strength of his powerful body against her own, feeling relief and a new warmth stealing over her like a gentle tide. It was all over; they were safe and she was here, in Nicolas's arms, at last!

She did not ask about Daphne until they were standing on the deck of the fishing boat heading for Norbos across the narrow strait of water which had separated them all through that terrible night.

'Daphne is no longer on the island,' he said grimly. 'She has gone to a photographic assignment in Rome, taking her mother with her as an afterthought, I imagine. They had something of an argument and then Kyria Caprodistrias agreed to go with her.'

'But—we saw *Swordfish* along the mole when we passed——'

'That was yesterday.' His arm tightened about her. '*Swordfish* has gone and Daphne and her mother with it, but Paris Xilas wants to come back later in the year to work on the excavations. He was with the German dig on Somthes some time ago and he is quite knowledgeable. He feels that our island might be equally interesting.'

'Our island!' His voice had been warm with affection as he uttered the words.

'You were still there,' she asked, 'after the museum was opened?'

'No.' His gaze went beyond her to the open sea. 'I went to Volponé. I wanted to speak to you alone, not just in a crowd, but when I got there they told me you had left for Karistos to join Michael. They told me you were going back to England and—somehow—I had to stop you doing that.'

'When did you know about the storm?' she asked.

'I saw it coming. I went back to Norbos hoping to find you sheltering there, but there was no sign of you so I began a search. I went in the wrong direction at first, towards Kea, but when there was no sign of you there I joined up with the fishermen who had put into harbour earlier than usual because of the storm. One boat had picked up a faint mayday call on its way in. We're standing on it now.'

'Nicolas, they're marvellous people!' She put her head against his shoulder, shyly at first, and then with more confidence. 'I'll always owe them so much.'

When they finally sailed into the quieter water along the mole, his own caique was moored safely there in the starlight. The fuller light of dawn had yet to appear over the eastern mountains, but they went ashore immediately, climbing up between the little cubic houses on to the plateau where they could see the villa standing out whitely among the cypress trees and the dome of the church shimmering palely against the darker stone of the ruined fortress crowning the precipice.

'We must phone through to Volponé as quickly as we can,' Nicolas said, helping her up the slope. 'Your grandfather is very anxious—naturally. He's also concerned about Ariana, who is known to do foolish things in an emergency.'

'Nicolas, she was wonderful!' Rhea declared. 'Calm and collected, really, for most of the time, and Michael being so down-to-earth helped a lot.'

'We'll get her back to Volponé as quickly as we can. Kyria Karousis is also very worried—about you both,' he added firmly. 'We all were.' He looked up towards the villa. 'My mother will be waiting for us.'

Alexandra Metaxas came from the open doorway of the villa as they crossed the courtyard.

'Thank God you are safe!' she said, drawing Rhea into her arms. 'We had all sorts of terrible thoughts during the night, but now you must come and get warm and have something to eat and drink. Then we will go to bed.'

The lamps were lit in the villa behind her, shedding a warm yellow glow out on to the portico where she had been waiting, but, tired though she was, Rhea knew that she would not sleep for a very long time. Her whole world had changed in the space of a few short minutes, in the time it had taken Nicolas to hold her in his arms.

When they were finally warmed and fed they gathered in the hall where a fire had burned for most of the day, and nobody seemed ready for sleep.

'I must phone Volponé,' Ariana said. 'I can't have them worrying about us till breakfast time.'

They all spoke in turn, assuring Phaedra and John Karousis that no harm had come to them, only to Michael's caique, and Michael made a little joke about it, saying that he would now have to buy a helicopter so that he could land wherever he liked.

'They'll be so relieved,' Alexandra said, yawning. 'And now I must go to bed and sleep till lunchtime!' She kissed Rhea on both cheeks, looking deeply into her eyes. 'Don't be too long before you come up, my dear. We will have so much to talk about tomorrow before we return to Athens.' She looked across the hall. '*Kalinikta*, Ariana! *Kalinikta*, Michael,' she added. 'Or should I wish you *Kaliméra* when it is so near the dawn?'

Ariana crossed the terrace to say good night to Michael, standing with him in the garden under the paling stars.

'You're tired.' Nicolas came close, holding Rhea by the shoulders to look down into her shining eyes. 'Tomorrow I will tell you how much I love you—how much I want you—and how I have been in love with you ever since I kissed you on the steps of the Tholos at Delphi.'

'Was I quite as transparent as that?' she challenged, remembering how passionately she had returned his first determined kiss. 'Could you read me so easily?'

'Not at all,' he said, 'but I have come to know you since, how generous you are and how loving. I know how much you cared for your father and how much you wanted the museum to be a success. Our two names are linked down there on the plaque, Rhea, and I want them to be linked for the rest of our lives, but we'll talk about all that tomorrow.' He bent his dark head to kiss her fully on the lips, holding her close for a long time before he let her go. 'Sleep well, darling,' he said, 'and I'll waken you when the sun is strong.'

Her eyelids felt heavy but she could not sleep while all this wonder was hers to hold for ever. A faint opal-coloured light was already staining the eastern sky, heralding a bright, clear dawn, and the wind that came with it was cool against their cheeks, but she clung to the hands he would have freed from her grasp, pressing his strong brown fingers to her lips.

'I want to see that dawn, however cold it is,' she told him. 'It will be like the beginning of a whole new life for me.'

'Our life,' he said, kissing her again. 'Our life together, Rhea. It could be no other way.'

The sun came up in a riot of colour, staining the surrounding sea in scarlet and gold as he led her back into the house his father had built for her mother all those years ago. It was another thing he would tell her in the morning.

ATTRACTIVE, SPACE SAVING BOOK RACK

Display your most prized novels on this handsome and sturdy book rack. The hand-rubbed walnut finish will blend into your library decor with quiet elegance, providing a practical organizer for your favorite hard-or soft-covered books.

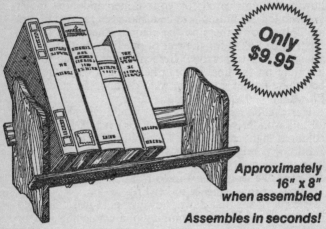

Only $9.95

Approximately 16" x 8" when assembled

Assembles in seconds!

To order, rush your name, address and zip code, along with a check or money order for $10.70* ($9.95 plus 75¢ postage and handling) payable to *Harlequin Reader Service*:

Harlequin Reader Service
Book Rack Offer
901 Fuhrmann Blvd.
P.O. Box 1396
Buffalo, NY 14269-1396

Offer not available in Canada.

BKR-1A

*New York and Iowa residents add appropriate sales tax.

The passionate saga
that began with SARAH continues in the compelling,
unforgettable story of

MAURA SEGER

In the aftermath of the Civil War, a divided nation—and two
tempestuous hearts—struggle to become one.

Available in December at your favorite retail outlet, or reserve your copy for November shipping by
sending your name, address, zip or postal code along with a check or money order for $4.70 (includes
75¢ for postage and handling) payable to Worldwide Library to:

In the U.S.

Worldwide Library
901 Fuhrmann Blvd.
Box 1325
Buffalo, NY 14269-1325

In Canada

Worldwide Library
P.O. Box 609
Fort Erie, Ontario
L2A 5X3

Please specify book title with your order.

 WORLDWIDE LIBRARY

ELI-1

Coming in April

Harlequin Category Romance Specials!

Look for six new and exciting titles from this mix of two genres.

4 Regencies—lighthearted romances set in England's Regency period (1811-1820)

2 Gothics—romance plus suspense, drama and adventure

Regencies

Daughters Four by Dixie Lee McKeone
She set out to matchmake for her sister, but reckoned without the Earl of Beresford's devilish sense of humor.

Contrary Lovers by Clarice Peters
A secret marriage contract bound her to the most interfering man she'd ever met!

Miss Dalrymple's Virtue by Margaret Westhaven
She needed a wealthy patron—and set out to buy one with the only thing she had of value....

The Parson's Pleasure by Patricia Wynn
Fate was cruel, showing her the ideal man, then making it impossible for her to have him....

Gothics

Shadow over Bright Star by Irene M. Pascoe
Did he want her shares to the silver mine, her love—or her life?

Secret at Orient Point by Patricia Werner
They seemed destined for tragedy despite the attraction between them....